Live-In Mum
LAURIE PAIGE

SILHOUETTE

SPECIAL EDITION ®

Silhouette, Silhouette Special Edition and Colophon are registered trademarks of Harlequin Books S.A., used under licence.

First published in Great Britain 1997
Large Print edition 1999
Silhouette Books Limited,
Eton House, 18-24 Paradise Road,
Richmond, Surrey TW9 1SR

© Olivia M Hall 1997

ISBN 0 373 59599 9

Set in Times Roman 16½ on 18 pt
35-9909-69726 C

Printed and bound in Great Britain
by Antony Rowe Ltd, Chippenham, Wiltshire

LAURIE PAIGE

reports romance is blooming in her part of Northern California. With the birth of her second grandson, she finds herself madly in love with three wonderful males—'all hero material'. So far, her husband hasn't complained about the other men in her life.

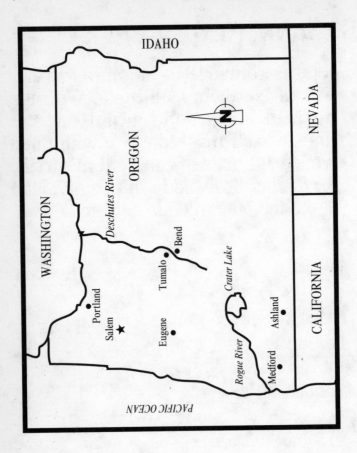

Chapter One

Carly Lightfoot sat straight up in bed. A rumble shook the walls of the frame ranch house. A major invasion apparently was taking place right outside the bedroom.

She leapt from the warm covers, rushed to the window and cracked the curtain an inch.

A jamboree of roaring trucks, bawling cattle, cursing cowboys and a barking dog milled around the stable yard, stirring up clouds of dust and a flock of bantam hens. The hens' indignant squawks added a comedic note to the early-morning ruckus.

Holding a shiver in by wrapping her arms across her chest, she stood on one foot, warming the left one on top of the right. She glanced at the sky. The sun wasn't up.

Elena, the cook for the ranch, had told her that cowboys started their days early. If this was an example of their usual work habits, she'd better get used to rising before dawn.

She dropped the curtain and dived under the warm covers, then contemplated the hours ahead of her. She lifted her arms toward the ceiling and arched her back in a lazy stretch.

Ah, the luxury of it, these hours of delicious idleness. No worries. No cares. No demands. Two whole days. All hers.

She knew what to do with them. Flinging the sheet and comforter aside, she dashed across the cold floor.

After a five-minute shower, she dressed and headed for the bunkhouse kitchen for breakfast before she set off to explore the fall foliage on the mountains that etched the border of the Macklin ranch, located in northern California near the Klamath River.

Dust invaded her nostrils as soon as she stepped outside. She sneezed three times and blinked when her eyes watered in irritation. Putting a bandanna over her nose, she blindly struck out across the stable yard, intent on reaching the safety of the kitchen before the next truck pulled up and unloaded its bellowing, unruly passengers.

Over the cacophony of cattle and chickens, she heard the cowboys raise their voices, shouting at each other, the cows and the deity that had brought them to this time and place.

She grinned behind the cotton protecting her nose and lungs from the dust. The pounding of hooves caused her to look up.

A cowboy on a huge black beast was heading straight for her. She stared at him, her mind blank with disbelief.

Before she could utter a single cry, he was upon her, intent on trampling her to death. She raised her arms defensively.

The next few seconds were a flurry of confused motion. She was swept up in a bruising embrace and thrust facedown over a saddle. She stared at faded denim, saddle stirrups, leather boots and the black, glistening hide of a horse.

A horn, long, pointed and dangerous, swept by a bare inch beneath her nose. She jerked her head upward as a dozen cattle charged to-

ward the open country, following the brindle
cow with the awesome rack of horns.

"Easy," a calm, masculine voice said. He
had the audacity to sound amused by the whole
thing. The large hand on her back pressed her
firmly against his thighs and the saddle horn.

He needn't have bothered. She was too
stunned to struggle.

Realizing she'd been saved from being
trampled by the renegade bunch of longhorns,
she let out her breath in a relieved whoosh and
tried to thank him at the same time.

The cowboy patted her back in a soothing
gesture.

Beneath her breasts and abdomen, she felt
the tensing of his thighs as he guided the horse
with his legs while one hand held her and the
other swung a coiled lariat at the running cattle.

"Please," she said, then realized he
couldn't possibly hear her plea to let her get
up and off this pounding beast before *all* her
ribs were cracked.

The black gelding continued his work, cutting this way and that as he turned the small

herd of mavericks toward the open gate of the pasture.

The constant jarring against her rib cage made breathing difficult. Blackness swirled into the dust eddies. For the first time in her life, she was going to faint. Helpless, she let her head sink until her chin bounced against her rescuer's knee.

"Hold on another minute," he said to her, bending over her and still swinging his rope. Leaning past her, he popped the leader of the runaway band on the shoulder. The big brindle hooked with those foot-long horns, coming dangerously close to the gelding's belly—and Carly's nose—before turning toward the gate. She bellowed her rage as she entered the enclosure, her ragtag followers on her heels.

The gate swung closed.

Carly's ears rang from the racket as she breathed in gasps. Her muscles strained with effort while she tried to keep from falling off headfirst. The gelding slid to a stop, doing a neat ninety-degree turn to keep from going through the gate after the cattle.

"By damn," someone said in admiration,

"that horse can turn on a dime and give back change."

"Ol' Painter knows his stuff," the cowboy who held her agreed.

Carly pushed herself off his thigh. "Help," she managed to gasp out before collapsing again.

An arm slipped between her and the saddle, wrapped itself around her directly under her breasts and hauled her upright. She was plopped sidesaddle across his lap, her left breast against his chest, her right one trapped under a broad palm.

Too shocked for words, she stared into the face of her knight in dusty denims.

"Easy," he said in soothing tones as if she were a nervous filly. He made sure she had her balance, then dropped his hand to the saddle horn, providing a backrest with his arm.

Ty Macklin looked into eyes as dark as the gelding's. He watched the shock of nearly being trampled evaporate like spit on a hot rock. Instead of anger or a dozen other emotions he'd learned to expect from a female, a flash of humor appeared in her eyes and the corner of her mouth dimpled.

Her hair was nearly as black as the horse he rode. It was shiny in the sun and shifted as she moved, each strand sliding past the others like a waterfall in slow motion. Fascinated, he stared as the breeze parted it on one side, then another as she turned her head to get it out of her eyes. The clean scent of shampoo and bath powder teased his nostrils.

As if he'd been there with her, he knew she'd gotten out of the shower minutes ago. He inhaled deeply, experiencing the flow of her scent into his lungs as a tactile pleasure.

He wondered what an early-morning ride would be like with her. In bed. With him as her mount. And her as his.

His blood pressure rose twenty notches. His body eagerly anticipated his musing by becoming heavy and turgid.

A ripple of surprise passed over him. He wasn't looking for trouble, and he knew it came in all sizes and shapes from Mae West voluptuous to tomboy slender. This woman was small, tiny waisted.

Size-ten trouble in a size-two dress.

Except she was wearing a shirt and jeans as faded as his, sneakers that were more holey than righteous, as his grandma used to say, and no bra. That much he knew.

His palms grew sweaty just thinking of that small but firm breast clasped under his hand. A perfect fit...

Hell and damnation. He had to get rid of those thoughts.

Carly took a shallow, shaky breath, inhaling the scent of him. Essence of Cowboy, she thought inanely. Dust, horses, cows, a spicy after-shave, all these, combined with the early-morning freshness of the mountain wind, enveloped her in the subtle caress of sensual pleasure. Her eyelids grew heavy as she gazed into his eyes and wondered what he was thinking.

He lifted one hand to resettle his hat while he studied her with an intensity that caused goose bumps to chase down her arms. His chest lifted in a quick breath while his heart increased its beat against her breast. The unmistakable feel of male arousal made her aware of him on several levels at once.

She felt something within herself coil tighter and tighter, then expand suddenly, a sensuous bloom of well-being that was as pleasant as it was surprising. If he'd ridden off with her at that moment, she'd have gone with him without question, done whatever he wanted for their mutual pleasure.

They sat that way, staring at each other, his eyes narrowing as if in suspicion, her own widening in confusion. She wasn't the type to ride off into the sunset with anyone.

Behind them, someone called a ''Yaiii, yaiii'' to the cattle being unloaded. A horse snorted. The dog, a mixed breed of boxer and shepherd, barked in sharp yips.

Her cowboy looked away, shifted in the saddle, then asked in a low drawl, ''Where you off to?''

''The kitchen.'' She ducked her head, shaken by the feelings rioting through her.

He clicked to the gelding. His thighs moved under hers as he guided the big horse to the edge of the porch at the bunkhouse. There, he set her on her feet, his hands exquisitely gentle.

She glanced up and saw him looking at her lips. When he licked his, she moistened hers, too.

As if they were getting ready to kiss.

She took her first deep breath in—was it only five minutes since she'd been swept across his saddle like a heroine in an old Western movie?—and winced.

"Are you all right?"

His voice was like a warm rain, vibrant with life and the promise of spring, belying the chill of mid-October and the early snow already on the tallest mountains peaks. She managed a wry grin. "Yes. Except for the broken ribs."

He grinned back at her.

"Hey, boss, you gonna sit there making cow eyes at that gal all day? What're we gonna do with these here beeves?"

The cowboy tipped his hat, then swung the reins against his mount's neck. The big horse took off with a giant bound, eager to get on with his work.

Carly lingered on the porch. To her eyes, the cowboy was the living portrayal of a demigod from Greek myth, one of those half mortals sired by a powerful Titan of ancient times.

The sun glinted from his eyes, which were the pure blue of the early-morning sky. His face glowed with health, its planes and hollows attractively defined by the play of light and shadow over him. Thick tawny hair spilled over his forehead, blown by the cool fall breeze.

He and the horse flowed together, moving as one, lithe… graceful…powerful….

Boss. Was he the foreman of the ranch?

Her heartbeat slowed to normal, and her breathing became regular. Turning toward the kitchen door, she relived the gentle strength of his arms around her, strength a woman could crawl into and be sheltered and cherished from life's barbs….

Sighing, she opened the screened door. She could use a bit of cherishing. She was here on the ranch to rediscover herself, to gain some breathing space and rethink her future.

Eighteen months ago, she'd broken up with her fiancé. The division of furniture and assets had taken one and a half years out of her life and a chunk out of her heart.

Her former beloved had also tried to claim a third of the successful trio of tiny gift boutiques she'd started and nourished to life on her own. The resulting lawsuit had left her exhausted and empty. She was here to replenish her soul.

She paused and looked back, drawn to her rescuer—her cowboy—in spite of warnings that rang inside. Was he a man who knew how to cherish? Maybe she'd find out. Smiling at her foolish musing, she went inside.

"Good morning," Elena called out. The cook plopped a platter of pancakes on the steam table.

"Good morning."

"You're just in time. Hurry and eat before the men finish with the cattle, else you might not get anything."

"I will. Thanks." Carly hurried across the room.

When her friend Isadora Chavez had insisted she come for a visit after the lawsuit was resolved—in her favor—she'd taken Isa up on the offer. At Isa's home, reading the Sunday paper, Carly had found out about a job here at the ranch. It seemed like the hideaway she needed.

She'd interviewed with a local sheriff, who was half owner, and swore Isa to secrecy about her whereabouts. Her ex-fiancé, who knew all her friends, kept calling. He seemed to think they could make up, get married and share the wealth.

The jerk.

She was glad she'd acted on the odd impulse, she mused as she surveyed the long room that served as the ranch kitchen, dining room and lounge. The ranch reminded her of her grandfather's place on Hopi land in Arizona. She'd felt happy and secure there.

Accepting the plate Elena handed her, she loaded it with three pancakes and a dipper of warm syrup. She conscientiously left off the butter in an effort to watch her fat intake, then added two slices of bacon to the plate. Oh, well.

''How long have you been up?'' she asked. Although she wasn't supposed to start to work for a couple of days, she felt a twinge of guilt that the cook, who looked younger than Carly's thirty years, seemed to be handling the meal alone.

No, she reminded herself. She wasn't responsible for the rest of the world. That was what had gotten her into that ill-fated engagement. From now on, she looked after *numero uno*.

"Since five. Did all the commotion wake you up? I forgot to tell you the cattle would be coming from the higher ranges all this week when you arrived yesterday."

Carly nodded. "I thought it was an invasion. Do they always truck the cows down?" she asked, confused about this aspect of ranch life. Or maybe she'd seen too many Westerns. Maybe cattle drives were a thing of the past.

Elena prepared a plate for herself and joined Carly at the end of a table long enough to seat twelve. "The cattle are brought in from mountain pastures up in Oregon."

"Oh."

Elena smiled kindly at her confusion. "The winters are too severe in the mountains. The cattle would die. The men bring the Macklin herd here, as well as some of the other ranchers' cattle."

She brought them each a cup of coffee and sat across the table. Her dark eyes were friendly, her smile warm.

Carly, with her tawny skin and black hair and eyes inherited from her Indian grandfather, was at ease with the other woman, who appeared to be Hispanic.

Except for one man, Pete Hodkin, who'd directed her to the bunkhouse when she'd arrived the previous day, she'd liked all the people she'd met so far.

Glancing around, she sighed with relief that Hodkin hadn't seen her arrival at breakfast and joined them. When she'd asked directions to the house, his smile had been insulting and snide as he looked her over. He'd sent her to Elena, who'd given her a room in the house where the cook also had quarters.

Her mind drifted past him to the cowboy who'd saved her from the runaway herd. Now *there* was a man.

An ache echoed dimly through her heart. She wasn't looking for a man, but he had been...interesting.

She dropped the line of thought. Being rescued by the cowboy didn't mean she had to fall for him. She could enjoy the moment for what it was—an interlude that had been scary and exciting at the same time.

A question in the back of her mind jostled itself to the front—would she like future contact with her sexy rescuer?

"What are your plans for the day?" Elena asked, giving her outfit a curious once-over.

Carly glanced down at her old clothes. She probably looked about twelve in her old jeans and shirt. But her cowboy hadn't thought of her as a child.

A stirring warmth spread through her. It was odd to feel this way about a man she'd just met.

Looking wasn't committing, she reminded herself. A person could shop around. That didn't mean she had to buy in to a line or vows of love. Besides, she would only be here for a month. That wasn't long enough to get seriously involved. By then, she'd have made up her mind about the future. She disliked uncertainty.

"I thought I'd ride over the hills and explore the ranch a bit. Is there someone I can ask for the loan of a horse?"

"Pete Hodkin. He handles the horses."

"Oh, him."

"*Sí*," Elena agreed.

Carly met the other woman's eyes. Understanding flashed between them. Yes, she was definitely going to like Elena.

She resumed eating. Her thoughts kept reverting to the cowboy and those brief moments of contact.

He'd been gentle with her after snatching her from danger. His lightning-fast reflexes had spared her possible harm. He'd been careful when he'd steadied her after the accidental caress that had left her burning with unexpected longing.

She wondered what he'd been thinking when he'd looked at her so intently before releasing her.

Recalling the contact of their bodies and the increased beating of his heart against her breast, she was pretty sure she knew. Electric tingles dashed around in her chest.

There had been awareness in his eyes. Then, like a door closing, it was gone. But when she'd looked back before entering the kitchen, he'd been looking her way.

She was certain he was feeling the tingles, too.

Hold it. She wasn't here for a fling with a good-looking cowboy, no matter how gentle or charming. She was here to relax and decide if she wanted to settle in the area.

She'd sold her business to her former manager, the sale final a month ago. She'd done the same with the condo. Now she was free to pursue greener pastures. She was considering a boutique in Ashland. The town did a nice tourist business.

When she saw Elena take her empty plate and put it in a sink filled with soapy water, she finished her meal and did the same.

Realizing there really weren't any other workers in the kitchen-dining room and that Elena was doing all the cooking and serving alone, Carly fought a battle with her conscience.

This was not her problem. She had two days to adjust to the new place.

Right, room and board while she lazed around and planned a glorious new life, her conscience scolded.

But she was supposed to be resting and thinking about things. She had a new business venture to consider.

So, she couldn't work and think at the same time?

When a half-dozen cowboys filed in and

heaped their plates high with food, she volunteered to help out.

"No, no, you're not supposed to start until Monday," Elena protested, but with a hopeful gleam in her eyes.

Carly shrugged. "So I'll charge overtime."

A working vacation was made to order to her way of thinking. She wasn't used to being idle. Living on a ranch and getting paid for it had seemed a perfect solution to her. She didn't mind starting a couple of days early. "What do you want me to do?"

They got a coffee break at nine. Carly eased her body down on a chair. She'd spent three hours washing dishes, mashing potatoes and peeling apples for pies. After lunch, there was dinner to prepare...after they washed dishes again.

"Have you people ever heard of this marvelous new invention?" she asked. "It's called a dishwasher."

Her companion snickered. Carly gave a weak grin. Even her face was tired.

"Cheer up," Elena advised, smiling in sympathy.

"Why? Are we quitting soon?"

"The usual time, three."

"As in this afternoon? I'll never make it."

Elena laughed as if Carly had told a really funny joke. She prepared two cups of coffee and brought one to Carly, along with a doughnut for each of them. A young man had already taken out coffee and a box of fresh pastries for the men.

"Cowboys eat a lot," Carly remarked, watching as several stopped their tasks with the cattle, washed their faces and hands at a spigot, then sat on the end of the porch to eat.

"This is a good place to work," Elena said. "Ty provides plenty of food. You'd better finish. We only have a few minutes."

Carly's arm trembled when she lifted the doughnut to her mouth. She couldn't remember why she'd thought working in a ranch kitchen was such a neat idea.

Maybe she could quit…no, she couldn't do that to Elena. The woman needed all the help she could get to feed the horde of men who worked on the ranch. If she ever met the younger brother of Shane Macklin, the sheriff, who was supposed to be running the ranch, she'd give him an earful about that.

Then he'd probably throw her off the place.

She rested her head against the back of the chair, closed her eyes and chewed slowly. Well, she'd simply refuse to leave. She'd taken this on for a month. Besides, she was here to find herself.

Whatever that meant.

Anyway, that was why she'd left Chicago and driven west, following the sun…and her friend's advice.

"Get out of town. Forget the past. Take a long vacation. You deserve it. You can stay with me and my brother. Bed and board as long as you want, all free. So what's holding you up?" Isa had demanded when they'd talked about it.

So she'd packed up, kissed Chicago goodbye, albeit a bit nostalgically, and headed for the Wild West.

She'd stopped to visit Isa, who was working two jobs—full-time theater manager and part-time actress—and having problems with her thirteen-year-old brother, up in southern

Oregon. Isa hadn't needed the complication of a guest.

Last Sunday, she'd seen the ad and succumbed to the lure of a working vacation on a real ranch.

"You're new at this kind of work, aren't you?" Elena asked after the silence had stretched to several minutes.

Carly opened her eyes and grinned wryly. "You noticed."

Elena laughed.

Meeting the other woman's eyes, she felt they were fast becoming friends. "So how long have you been cooking for the crew of the Rocking M outfit?"

"Ten years, but I'm only here for two months a year."

Carly was startled. "You must have started when you were a mere babe. You can't be older than I am."

"I'm twenty-eight. I'm saving for my little ones to go to college," Elena explained proudly.

"You have children?"

"Yes. Three girls. They will go to the university and become teachers and not get married too soon like I did.''

''Who's with your girls?''

''My mother lives with us each winter. I start cooking when the cows are moved down to the winter pastures and we have so many men to feed. At Thanksgiving, I go home, then return in spring when the cattle are moved to high pastures.''

''Where's home?''

Elena finished her treat and stood. ''Near Redding. My husband works in the lumber mill. We'd better get to work, or dinner will be late.''

''Not to mention lunch.'' Carly licked her fingers, drank the rest of the coffee and headed for the kitchen, which was tucked behind a counter and cabinets at one end of the long room.

Elena got there first. ''I'll start a stew for the men's supper. They clean up after themselves at night. Lunch is the main meal of the day. We call it dinner on the ranch. You can peel potatoes, if you like.''

''Sure. That has to be better than washing a mountain of dishes. We've got to see about some modern appliances for this ranch. Dishwasher first, automatic peeler second. Surely someone has invented one by now.''

Elena seemed to think everything she said was hilarious. The young cook was still chuckling as she started making up the pies for lunch. Dinner. Or supper. Whichever.

Carly's relief was short-lived. She found it didn't matter how she squirmed. The same motion, repeated hundreds of times, was exhausting. She looked out the window, wondering if it had been a good thing to take on this job.

She groaned. It wasn't even lunch yet. She picked up another potato and sighed.

''Here comes the boss man,'' Elena sang out. She didn't sound worried. In fact, there was a smile in her voice.

''So you returned for another year,'' a pleasant baritone stated. ''I thought you vowed never to cook for a bunch of ill-mannered cowboys again last spring.''

Elena laughed and shook her head. ''The pay is good. And I expect a *big* bonus.''

''And here I thought you returned every year because of my charm,'' the man said, heaving a loud sigh of disappointment.

Carly peeked up to see if this was truly the man who'd given her a case of chill bumps merely by looking at her after his rescue that morning. It was, and she still got them.

"That's the real reason, but my husband doesn't know," her partner informed him.

Elena's voice became musical, the slight Spanish accent more pronounced as she spoke to the cowboy. The foreman? Carly wished she'd asked more about the ranch and its operations.

The man was enough to turn any woman's head. His smile was a white slash against his tanned face. With his shirt open to the waist, she could see sweat glistening in the patch of tawny hair on his chest. His torso rippled with muscles as he shifted his weight. She imagined how it would feel to touch him, to run her fingers along that warm, moist flesh, to taste the salty tang left on his skin by his labor....

He stepped forward, and his eyes met hers. She gazed at him, held captive by his intensity. Although he continued to smile, she sensed something else in him, a question.

She bore his scrutiny for a long minute, then turned away and started to work with a flurry of renewed energy. This man created entirely too much havoc with her senses. She kept her back toward the other two, hoping he would leave soon.

No such luck.

"This the new helper?" he asked.

"Yes. Carly Lightfoot. Carly, this is the boss," Elena introduced them. "When I spoke to Shane, he said he would send someone as soon as possible. I didn't expect her the next day. She is a very good worker. But not as good as me."

His soft chuckle washed over Carly. Why was it that his very presence made her as dizzy as riding a double-loop roller coaster at the fair?

He moved closer. Doggedly, she went on peeling the potato while she fought the insane notion to run her hands over him.

"If you peel that much more, we'll have to eat the skins to get any nourishment," he advised.

She dropped the abused vegetable into the bucket.

He plucked a red-and-gold-speckled pear from a bowl on the counter and took a big bite.

"Delicious," he murmured. "Sweet and crisp. A bit of tartness to add spice. It's a new type of pear from the orchards. The Macklin pear. See what you think of it."

His voice was low, mellow, but with a slight grittiness that caused heat to slide down her spine. He wasn't talking about a piece of fruit.

His gaze went to her mouth. She thought of his lips on hers, of the tangy taste of the pear coming to her tongue from his. Before she could retreat from these sensuous thoughts, he held the pear to her mouth so she had to take a bite.

The crunch of her teeth sounded like a horse chomping corn in the silent room. Both the foreman and Elena watched her for a reaction. She chewed and swallowed.

"It's very good. Thank you." She was going to taste *him* if he didn't get out of the kitchen and her vicinity. She'd never been hungry for a man before, but looking at this one...

He studied her face. "Have I seen you before?" he queried.

"You saved me from the stampede earlier today."

He took another bite from the pear. "Yes, but before that? You look familiar."

"No," she said. "This is my first visit here." She took the bucket of potatoes to the sink to rinse them, wondering why her inner warning system wasn't clanging like mad.

Elena washed her hands after lining twelve pie pans with dough. When she moved aside, Carly stayed at the sink and started cleaning carrots.

"You'd better put on an apron. You're splashing water on your shirt," her cowboy advised. He reached into the open door of the walk-in pantry and lifted an apron from a hook.

He proceeded to slip the loop over her head, then caught the ties on each side and pulled them into a bow at her back. Every touch sent little points of fire through her shirt. It was a wonder she didn't burst into flames. When he finished and said goodbye, then left, she sagged with relief.

Some disdainer of men she was. If she was going to have a nervous breakdown every time the foreman came around, she might as well wear a sign that said Pushover.

Groaning silently at the thought, she turned to Elena. "I don't think you mentioned the foreman's name."

"Foreman?" Elena shook her head. "We don't have a foreman. The boss handles the ranch himself."

"The boss?"

"The man who was here. That was Ty Macklin. Sorry. I thought you knew." She gave Carly a speculative glance.

Ty Macklin. Isa had told her about him. His wife had divorced and left him with their son to raise. His son had had leukemia and nearly died before the boy's aunt donated bone marrow to save his life.

The boss might have money and charm, but it didn't sound as if his life had been all that rosy.

No. She was not going to feel sorry for Ty Macklin. Most marriages broke up for a reason, also engagements.

She'd found her fiancé in the arms of someone else, telling the woman the same sob story about his orphaned youth and unhappy childhood that he'd used on her.

From now on, she dealt with men with her head, not her heart.

She attacked a carrot with the peeler and soon had the pound pack done. A companionable silence fell on the kitchen while she worked at the sink and Elena put the pies in to bake.

Yeah, it was nice working with Elena. Four weeks of working on a ranch wasn't a bad way to spend a vacation.

If she could keep herself away from Ty Macklin.

Chapter Two

Ty Macklin strode toward the stable. The cattle were settling in the pastures behind the hay barn. The men would move them to other fields during the next few days, after they'd been checked for pinkeye, worms and other parasites.

There was a lot of work to do. He couldn't stand around all day, his mind on the cook's helper like some teenager with rampant hormones.

He walked up a row of oak trees and into the barn, where a couple of hands worked on a horse, treating it for a sore foot. He tossed the rest of the pear to the gelding he'd ridden that day.

"Hey, boss, look at this," Hodkin, the man in charge of the horses, called.

He walked over and checked the hoof, which was cracked. The frog was bruised and inflamed.

"Bad, huh?" Hodkin commented.

"Yeah. Clean it good and rest him until it heals." Ty pushed back his hat and glanced at the other cowhand.

It took some getting used to, but this was the second female wrangler who had worked there. The gal from last year had gotten married and was expecting a child. She'd recommended her cousin Venita to take her place.

Ty gave her an encouraging smile. She wasn't like Elena's new helper, the black-haired Venus who had returned his gaze as bold as the fox who lived in the woods on the ridge west of there.

He went outside and gazed at the cattle. They were a new cross he was trying—a French breed mixed with Texas longhorn. He wondered if he could mix them with polled Hereford and produce a hardy breed with no horns. Or at least a bit shorter than those of the big brindle who'd nearly hooked the new kitchen hand.

His body reacted as it had earlier, growing hot and heavy in his britches. She'd felt good in his arms, sweet smelling and womanly. He shrugged impatiently and walked on.

Near the line of oaks that served as a windbreak, he paused to chat with old Martha, who was the general housekeeper for the ranch. She and her sister were married to his two best ranch hands and lived on the place all year.

"Ty, you married yet?" Martha demanded, glancing up from her task, then going back to it without missing a sheet.

"No," Ty assured the nearly toothless matron, "I'm waiting for you to get rid of your old man."

"I'm gonna keep him, but my granddaughter..." She rolled her eyes and made clicking sounds with her tongue. "She's one beauty, that one, just out of high school and looking for trouble."

"Martha wants to get the girl married off so she can quit worrying about her," Mary, the sister, volunteered. She gave a cackle of laughter and went back to hanging clothes.

Ty had bought Martha a dryer to go with the new washer, but the older woman insisted sunshine not only dried the bedclothes but "purified" them, as well.

Martha bobbed her head, gray hair wafting around her merry face. She gave Ty a sly grin. "That's right. Let the husband keep her busy at night, the children can keep her busy in the day, then she'll be too tired to get into mischief."

Ty grinned, used to their ribald teasing. A picture of a slender backside and shapely legs clad in faded jeans came to him. "She didn't hire on as the new cook's helper, did she?" he asked, recalling dark, bold eyes. The new hand could be Hispanic.

Martha sniffed eloquently. "She is educated," she informed him. "She can type, and she knows computers."

"Give her a job in the office," Mary suggested. "You need someone to help with the paperwork. Buck said you've been behind for months."

Nothing was sacrosanct among these

women, he thought, feeling both irritation and affection. They'd worked at the ranch before his time. They'd probably be there after he was long gone. And they knew every damned thing that happened in the house or office.

"Send her around. I might be able to use her for a while."

"Then you can give her a letter to recommend her so she can get a better job," Martha said with evident satisfaction.

"Right." Grinning, he moved on, part of his mind overseeing the many operations going on around the ranch, part on the female who'd nearly gotten run down that morning.

She'd looked familiar, but he hadn't been able to put a memory to that piquant face. Nah, they'd never met before. He'd remember if he had. Carly Lightfoot. It didn't ring any bells, but that face...damn, he could swear he'd seen it before.

She had a small, sharp chin and high cheekbones. Her eyes were dark as obsidian. Her hair had fallen forward over her head when he'd hauled her across the saddle.

He'd wanted to kiss her neck.

In the kitchen, when she'd turned her back

on him and continued to work as if her life depended on it, he'd had to fight a strong urge to take her into his arms and do just that.

The delicate curve of that slender nape, or perhaps the way she held her head, had struck him as valiant and vulnerable at the same time. It reminded him of his son, Jonathan, who was also valiant and vulnerable....

He shook his head, perplexed at his own thoughts.

One thing for sure—he wasn't going to get mixed up with a woman again, not in any serious way. The only good thing to come out of his former marriage had been Jonathan. The six-year-old was visiting his mother and her new, very rich husband at the present, but he lived with Ty the rest of the year.

He wished his son were home, filling the empty rooms and long evening hours with his laughter and incessant questions.

Feeling lonely, old man? Yeah, he was. His thoughts returned to the woman.

Something about her bothered him. He grimaced. Yeah, holding her, smelling her sweet scent, feeling her warmth cradled against his—

those things were guaranteed to bother any normal male.

Whatever it was, it had him thinking of her the rest of the morning. He stayed in a state of partial arousal the whole time. By noon, he was thoroughly disgusted with his lack of control.

Had he expected to be immune to female charms forever? It had been over two years since his divorce, more than that since he'd been with a woman. He and his wife hadn't been exactly lovey-dovey the last months of their marriage.

His ex-wife had been rather lush, but this woman wasn't. Carly. He said the name to himself, liking it.

She was of average height and very slender. Her hips had curved nicely, though, below a waist that was tiny. And her breasts had felt damned good against his chest and under his hand when he'd accidentally touched her.

A burning sensation zigzagged through him. Each time he recalled that incident, a flame of need shot deep into his abdomen. Yeah, it had been a long time since he'd had a woman. As a single father, he'd become a saint.

Well, he didn't have time to dwell on that fact. Right now, he had several thousand head of cattle to worry about.

Carly trudged after Elena to the frame house. The main house was over the rise beyond a stand of trees, she'd learned. That was where Ty Macklin lived with his son.

She and Elena had set out lemonade and cookies after lunch, washed the dishes, finished the preparations for supper and were free the rest of the day. The remuda wrangler, much to Carly's relief, hadn't been around to eat so far. One of the men had told them there were a few problems with the horses.

Carly also learned there was another female at the house, a wrangler. In the bunkhouse, the men stayed in a big room off the dining room, each within his own partitioned space, while the females shared the frame house. Except for old Martha and Buck, plus Mary and her husband, all the help was temporary.

"Is it the usual practice to keep men and women separated?" she asked her partner.

Elena shrugged. "It is at this place. At others, they don't care. But I think it's better this way.''

''Better?''

''Yes. With men and women away from their families, it gets very lonely. You understand?''

''Yes. Of course.''

Carly understood loneliness. Her parents had been killed in an accident. While they were changing a tire on the side of the road, another driver had run into them. Her mother had put Carly out of harm's way well up the side of the bank, but then she'd gone to stand behind the car to talk to her husband while he jacked the rear wheel up.

The eight-year-old orphan had been passed around from relative to relative until a maiden aunt, actually her great-aunt, had taken her in and raised her. Her life had been fine after that, but those three years of drifting around, of not having a real home... It had been a hard life for a kid.

A tremor of emotion tore through her. Yeah, she knew about loneliness. Maybe that's why she'd been an easy mark later.

During high school and afterward, she'd

worked as many jobs as she could and hadn't had time for dates. After that, she'd been too busy starting her own business to see anyone. Then she'd fallen for a man who'd seen her as a quick way to get into business without working for it. Welcome to the real world.

She shuddered, thinking of her narrow escape.

Since then, she'd vowed to keep her eyes open, her heart shut and her nose to the proverbial grindstone. At thirty, she was no longer susceptible to the wiles of the heart...although Ty Macklin did make hers beat a little faster.

All right, a lot faster. So what?

Elena paused before a polished oak door. ''Sheets are in this cupboard when you need them. Martha and her cousin do the laundry twice a week. I have a marker pen to initial your things.''

She excused herself, went down the hall and collapsed on the bed in her room. Carly perused the living quarters. The long, narrow room was decorated with sturdy, comfortable furniture. A lamp was mounted on the wall above a small chest of drawers that served as a night table. The curtains crisscrossed over window shades of the type Aunt Essie had liked, the pull-down kind with a tasseled string attached.

Homesickness wafted over her.

It had been years since she'd felt it or allowed herself to think about the home where she'd finally found happiness. She wished she could see her great-aunt once more and listen to her practical advice on life. But Aunt Essie was gone, and Carly was on her own. She didn't like being rootless, yet she hadn't wanted to stay in Chicago. She'd find her place in the sun soon.

She rose and took another quick shower, then dressed in blue slacks with a long-sleeved sweater of blue and beige stripes. The days were warm, but the nights were chilly in this area.

Elena was in the living room when she returned. ''The stew should be done now. You can eat any time you're ready. We often go outside when the weather is nice.''

They watched the news on TV. Later she went with Elena to the ranch dining room. Carly had thought she was too tired to eat, but smelling the stew, she realized she was ravenous.

When their plates were heaped to overflowing, she and Elena grabbed glasses of iced tea and headed outside. Fifty yards from the bunkhouse, a path opened into a meadow beside the river.

Picnic tables, their benches already filled with chatting workers, dotted the area.

A wolf whistle sounded behind Carly as she and Elena headed for the river. Glancing around, Carly realized the whistle was for her. She kept her chin up and tried not to look self-conscious.

Elena chose a quiet spot beside the swiftly flowing water. She and Carly sat on the grass, their backs against two boulders.

"Did you take those other painkillers?" Elena asked. She'd given Carly two pills at lunch and two for later.

"I forgot." Carly dug the tablets out of her pocket and washed them down with a swallow of iced tea.

"You've been a true lifesaver today. I really appreciate it," Elena told her. "It would have taken me much longer to do all the work by myself.''

Carly waved her thanks aside. They ate in silence.

When she'd finished every last bite, she sighed and leaned her head on the rock. She may have had softer pillows, but none had ever felt so welcome as this one, she mused, smiling at her naive concept of what ranch work really meant.

She heard Elena stir, but didn't open her eyes. She didn't think she could. She was so sleepy. Someone might have to carry her to bed. A picture of Ty Macklin came to mind.

Not him, she warned herself. Not the boss.

He was a man to turn a woman's heart with his laughter and teasing ways. With a failed marriage behind him, he probably wasn't looking for a permanent connection any more than she was. Who knows? Maybe they would be good for each other.

Isa had said he'd been drinking a lot back when his marriage was going to hell in a hand basket. Carly wrinkled her nose in distaste. That was one problem she'd steer clear of. She didn't need involvement with someone who couldn't handle his life better than that.

Besides, he had poor taste in women if what Isa had said about his wife was true. The woman had been a blond beauty, spoiled, petulant and out for what she could get. She had given Ty a really rough time. Maybe he'd deserved it.

"Where is your family?" Elena asked, sitting again after taking their plates and forks to the kitchen.

"I'm it," Carly said, opening her eyes and watching the river, feeling rather melancholy about life. "My parents are dead. I was raised by a maiden aunt."

"You had no brothers or sisters?" Elena asked, her brown eyes warm with sympathy.

"I had a foster brother while I was growing up. Brody is my family now." She grinned affectionately, thinking of the other orphan her great-aunt had taken in. He was older than she was and quite protective. He'd threatened to break her former fiancé's handsome nose until she'd told him the jerk wasn't worth it.

The sound of laughter, male laughter, delivered in a baritone with a slight grittiness, brought her wide-awake. She glanced over her shoulder. Ty Macklin stood by one of the tables, talking to some of the cowboys. He had a full plate in his hand.

His eyes met hers. Gazing into them was like being engulfed in a pure blue sky. All day, she thought irrationally, she'd wished for the hours to speed by as she worked; now she wished time would stand still—

"Elena, introduce me to your friend," a cheerful male voice demanded, bringing Carly's attention to the immediate present with a neck-jarring snap.

A young man stood in front of them, his feet braced apart, his shirt open down the front although the air was cooling rapidly. He had his hands tucked into his hip pockets while he brashly surveyed her with open appreciation.

From the corner of her eye, she saw the other men watching them, the younger ones grinning, the older ones with a frown of disapproval. Undercurrents that she didn't understand ruffled her composure. She took a firm grip on herself.

Elena shook her head. "Go away, Rodrigo."

Carly was surprised at the rebuke in Elena's tone. As an observer of human nature, she was at once interested in the young lothario, wondering what he'd done to draw the older people's ire.

"Then I will do it myself," he announced grandly. "I am Rodrigo Diaz."

"I'm Carly Lightfoot."

Rodrigo plopped down on the grass. "I haven't seen you before today. You're new in this area?"

"Yes."

"Don't trouble yourself with this one," Elena broke in. "He is a flirt. He comes on to all the girls."

He laid a hand over his chest. "Elena broke my heart long ago. I console myself as best I can."

Carly grinned. She could see he was a flirt, but a harmless one. Mostly he was full of himself, as her great-aunt would have said. He was good-looking and confident of his charm, but in an easygoing way. She liked him. "Are you a cowboy?"

His chest puffed up a bit. "I am studying land management."

"Oh." She was impressed. "So what do you do?"

"Soil testing. Spraying. Fertilizing. The pastures require care all year long."

Elena stood. "I'm going to talk to Martha."

When she left, another young man came over. He helped with the horses and was learning to be a blacksmith. His name was William, and, like her, he was new at the ranch.

The two young men showed off for her, trying to outboast each other and impress her with the importance of their respective positions. She laughed at their antics.

Once, when she laughed, she saw Ty turn his head toward her. He hadn't glanced her way since that first moment until now. He finished his conversation with the older men and came over.

"It's time to go in," he advised. "In case you want another piece of pie for a bedtime snack, you'd better get it."

Rodrigo looked toward the open door to the kitchen, then back to her. It was obvious he was torn by his desire for a treat and his determination to stay with her.

She made it easy for him. ''I think I'll go to my room and read for a while.''

''I'll walk with you,'' Ty volunteered, stopping the same words obviously on the lips of the younger men. ''I want to explain about your hours.''

The flash of surprise on the other two faces confirmed her suspicion that the hours on a ranch were those necessary to get the work done. Ty wanted to see her alone.

She felt a tiny surge of uneasiness at going off into the twilight with him, but couldn't detect any emotion in her boss's face as they walked across the grass. However, he looked rather grim as he went into the kitchen to wash and store his dishes.

She cleaned her plate and glass and walked toward the frame house. Ty followed behind. The other workers were silent until they'd departed, then she heard the murmur of a dozen conversations start up behind them.

At the patch of lawn in front of the house, he stopped her. ''Your behavior is inappropriate,'' he said.

Astonishment was her first reaction. ''I beg your pardon?''

"Those are young guys and they're lonely. They were raised in a stricter culture than we have here. When Elena went over to the other women, you should have, too."

"You don't say," she murmured, her hackles rising. He might be the boss, but he had no right to tell her how to act.

He cast her a glance that would have turned a coyote to stone. "Your staying with them was provocative. When you laugh and talk with them alone, they think you're giving them the green light."

"You've got to be kidding. In case you people haven't noticed, these are modern times. Besides, I'm hardly the type to drive men wild," she scoffed.

One dark brow—an enticing contrast to the tawny hair—rose sarcastically at this statement. "You're sexy as hell…and you damned well know it." If grimness came in degrees, he looked close to the nth stage of it.

"Well," she said, taken aback by his declaration. He thought she was sexy. As hell! Peering into his eyes, she saw no signs of it in his expression.

He folded his arms across his chest. Fascinated, she watched the play of muscle under the flesh and recalled how strong he'd felt when he'd held her for those moments out of eternity.

"I want you to stay away from the men," he announced.

The delicate bud of pride that had sprouted when he said she was sexy withered under his fierce glare. He acted as if she were some Lolita out to drive men mad with desire.

She lifted her chin. "The last I heard, this was a free country. I choose my own friends."

His smile startled her, until she realized it was more like a snarl. "Not on Macklin land. You'll do as you're told, or you can find another job."

"You can't fire me for what I do on my own time." She stuck her nose up and smiled right back.

"But I can fire you for sexual harassment," he murmured, his tone dropping to a low threat.

For a second, his words didn't make sense. When they did, she burst out laughing. "That's the most absurd thing I ever heard."

"Is it?" He took a step toward her.

His physical warmth invaded the front of her body, then encircled her like a lover's caress. She became aware of her own physical nature in a way that she hadn't been conscious of in a long time. The need to touch, to share caresses, became overpowering. It was the oddest thing....

A shudder tore through her. Warnings clanged in her head like a five-alarm fire. Before she could react, his hands settled on her shoulders.

She stared at him, unable to believe what she saw in his eyes. But she wasn't mistaken. He lowered his head, his intent clear.

He meant to kiss her.

Her own eyes closed involuntarily, the lids too heavy to hold open when his mouth brushed across hers, warm and slightly moist.

When he moved away, she licked her lips and found the taste of him—a tangy blend of the lemonade he'd been drinking and the subtle, spicy flavor of his mouth—on them.

He didn't give her time to retreat. Instead, he took another kiss, this time moving swiftly between her surprised, parted lips to claim her mouth, driving out any protest she might have made.

A flash of agony, of some strange desire stronger than any she'd ever known, surged through her. Her legs went weak with it. She locked her arms around his waist, needing his help to stay upright under the onslaught of this fierce passion.

Dimly, she knew his intensity was made up of anger as much as anything else. And perhaps frustration that she'd laughed at his warning. Then her thoughts faded into a rosy haze as he moved even closer, his chest rising and falling in quick breaths against hers.

She'd never known human contact could feel so wonderful, so honestly, sweetly right, as his hands roamed her back.

His tongue invaded her mouth again. She answered each moist caress with one of her own, spellbound by all that was happening.

Abruptly, he tore himself from her, stepping back a foot and holding her when she would have instinctively followed.

''Hellfire,'' he muttered hoarsely. ''What *is* this?''

He sounded as if he'd discovered some phenomenon that no amount of logical thinking could explain.

"I don't know, but it was wonderful."

The wonder went out of him. His face hardened to the ferocity of an enraged eagle. "Now do you see?" he demanded.

"No."

Giving her a look of pure disgust, he stalked off toward the dark woods. "And from now on, wear a bra," he tossed back over his shoulder, and marched grimly off into the twilight.

She recovered her wits before he was completely out of sight. "From now on, don't touch me," she yelled at his back.

When she turned to stomp inside the house, she faced Elena and the three other women, who looked as shocked as she felt. She nodded to them and headed for her room, thankful for the privacy it provided.

Carly sighed tiredly on Friday. Ty had hurt her position with the other women by walking her to the house. Or maybe it was her own stubborn friendliness with Rodrigo.

Anyway, Elena had changed. She wasn't exactly cool, but neither was she as friendly as she'd been when they'd first met. A shadow of constraint had edged their conversation all week.

She grimaced. The women weren't sure of her relationship with the boss. Neither was she. Although he'd stayed away from her, she'd been aware of his presence in and around the ranch each day.

To her surprise, he was a hard worker, taking an active hand in moving bales of hay, checking on the condition of the cattle in the fields or deciding what fields to graze next.

From Isa's description of his life with his former wife, Carly had concluded Ty Macklin was a playboy type. Now she found she had to revise that opinion.

Her muscles tensed when she heard him laughing with the men at the stables. He was quiet when he approached the porch where she and Elena sat shucking corn. He checked the huge pot after nodding to them.

"Are you two going to work tomorrow?" he asked.

"I am." Elena glanced over at Carly. "We get extra for working on Saturday."

Carly hoped the erratic pounding of her

heart wasn't as loud as it seemed to her. "Well, I hadn't planned on it." At his sharp glance, she added defensively, "I have things to do."

Things like planning her future. She wasn't making much progress. Not that the work kept her from thinking. No, it was just that, for the first time in years, she felt...at peace.

She didn't understand the feeling. Tomorrow, she was going to drive up to Ashland and visit Isa. Maybe her friend could give her some advice on starting a new boutique.

"We'll knock off at three tomorrow," he told Elena. "Martha said they're having a cookout at six, if you want to join them." His glance took in Carly, too.

"My husband is coming up with my girls," Elena told him.

"You know they'll be welcome."

Elena smiled happily. The two women worked silently after he left. Carly heard Elena sniff a time or two. The third time, she peeked and saw her friend wipe her eyes.

"What's wrong?" she asked. "Are you hurt?"

"No." Elena shook her head and laughed a

little. "I don't know what's worse—not seeing my family for a month or seeing them and knowing they will be gone in a few hours."

"I understand," Carly murmured sympathetically.

A sudden memory came to her. After her parents died, she'd sometimes stood by the window, staring down the road, praying that they'd come to get her and take her home. Knowing that it could never happen hadn't stopped her from longing for it.

When she'd become engaged, she'd allowed her dreams to revive. She'd thought they would marry and have a home, a family. It came to her she'd wanted those things more than she'd ever wanted the man. Gazing over the pastures, she thought of how wonderful it must be to have roots buried deep in this beautiful land....

Inside, a clock struck the hour. "Three o'clock," Elena announced. "We'll put these in the oven to roast. With ham and potato salad and green beans, that should do the men for supper."

With a tired but grateful sigh, Carly emptied her bucket and carried the corn shucks to the compost pile at the back of the stable. One week down. Three to go. She'd better get serious about scouting out locations for her boutique and sizing up the market. "Do we get paid today?" she asked.

Elena gave her a surprised glance. "Of course. Didn't they tell you?"

"I forgot to ask," she admitted.

The other woman shook her head, then smiled. "How have you gotten along in the world without someone to see to you?"

"I always find people like you to keep me informed." She laughed at her friend's look of exasperation. Elena's musical tones chimed in with no hesitation. Carly was relieved as they slipped back into easy companionship.

"We'll go to the office," Elena explained, leading the way. "You'll get paid for six days. Today, also tomorrow for those of us who work the extra day, will be paid next week."

"I see. Who pays us?"

Elena rolled her expressive eyes. "Come, child. Mama Elena will show you."

They were paid by check, it turned out. Martha, who seemed capable of running the ranch, had her sign a roster before handing the slip of paper over.

As she walked to her quarters, she looked at the signature at the bottom of the check. Ty Macklin had strong, clear handwriting. The check was drawn on a company account— Macklin Enterprises—on a bank in Yreka, the town closest to the ranch. Yreka was a thirty-minute drive along a winding road.

After she was showered and dressed, she paused outside Elena's room. "Knock, knock," she said.

Elena came out. She looked surprised to see Carly in a skirt and blouse. "You have a date?"

"No such luck," Carly denied. "I, uh, will probably be gone most of the weekend. I'm going to spend the night in Ashland with a friend."

"Girl or boy friend?" Elena demanded, her eyes twinkling.

"Wouldn't you like to know?" Carly assumed a supercilious expression, then ruined it with a rueful grimace. "No boyfriends," she lamented.

"Not even..." Dramatic pause. "Ty Macklin?"

Heat seeped into Carly's ears, and she wondered if her face had turned red. "Alas, no."

She hadn't tried to explain that strange kiss the women had witnessed. How could she when she couldn't explain it to herself? However, it had stayed on her mind all week. At times while she'd been working, heat would sweep through her body like a surge of hot lava, then she would realize she was thinking of him and that kiss.

No caress had ever affected her with the depth and suddenness of that one. She'd sensed raw, hungry passion, restrained anger and an unspoken need, all rolled into one.

"Well, I've got to go. See you later." She left, aware of curious glances from the other women.

Her car was pulled to the side of the driveway. She unlocked the door and opened it. The trapped heat spilled over her. She paused before getting into the stuffy interior.

"Say, you going to town?" William crossed the road. He was a tall, skinny young man, with sandy brown hair that fell in a straight lock over his forehead. He had a nervous habit of pushing it back. He stopped at the rear of the car. "I could use a lift."

She hesitated, wary of being alone with the cowboy after Ty's warning. "Uh, where do you want to go?"

"Downtown Yreka." He grinned at his joke. Downtown was about three blocks long.

"Okay." She got in and reached across the seat to unlock the passenger door.

After William was settled, she followed the winding road to the town. "Where to?" she asked.

"Just drop me in front of Smitty's right down the street." He pointed the place out to her.

She pulled into a side street and stopped beside the small market, which had a pool table, deli and bar at one side of the long room. She recognized the remuda wrangler. He was seated at a table near the windows with two other men.

A shiver of distaste pulsed through her. A week working at the ranch hadn't changed her mind about the man. There was something about him that reminded her of a reptile—the way his eyes followed her when she went outside or when he came into the dining room to eat and watch her at her work.

Following the main street, she came to the ramp and was soon speeding along Interstate 5. She noticed a sheriff's car on the shoulder of the road and recognized Shane Macklin, who was talking to a truck driver. The sheriff had the same thick tawny hair that Ty had. It was easy to see that the men were brothers. Shane was a couple of years older.

A bit farther down the road, she took the first exit and drove to her friend's home. Things were chaotic inside.

"We need a fill-in," Isa told her, throwing clothes and makeup in a bag. "I'm taking over the lead. Want to do a bit part? It's only four lines, but you'd get to be on stage most of the first act. Maybe you'll be discovered."

"No, thanks. If I walked out on a stage and saw hundreds of people staring at me, I'd faint dead away."

She nearly did when just one man with sky blue eyes and a smile to tempt a saint's heart looked at her. She pressed a hand against her chest, worried about the state of her own unstable organ.

Chapter Three

Ty parked in front of Shane's house, then, following his nose, walked around the flagstones to the back. His brother was standing over the grill, long-handled fork in hand.

"Yo," Shane called out. "Chicken's almost ready."

"Great. I'm starved."

Shane gave him a critical once-over, but he didn't comment. Ty had lost weight during the divorce. He hadn't managed to gain much of it back. Shane, on the other hand, had put on a pound or two since his marriage. Ty felt a pang of envy.

Shane and Tina adored each other. They

were generous with their love. It had expanded to cover him and Jonathan, too.

The door opened, and Tina came out, carrying a tray with tall glasses and a pitcher of iced tea. Ty crossed the patio in three strides and took it from her.

"Ty," she said warmly. "You're just in time."

"Why didn't you call me or Ty to carry the tray?" Shane demanded, clearly exasperated.

"It wasn't heavy." She went to her husband and leaned against his arm, not minding his scowl at all. She kissed his chin and smiled up at him.

Ty felt as if a frog had set up house in his throat. He cleared it and asked Tina how she felt. She'd told him earlier that summer, at Jonathan's sixth birthday party, that she was pregnant. At six months, it was evident.

"Fine. No more false labor."

"It wasn't false," Shane reminded her.

"Well, it went away."

Ty remembered how worried Shane had been when Tina had gone into labor earlier that month. She'd stayed in the hospital for a few days, taking some kind of medicine through an

IV before the doctor had decided she could come home. Ty'd been scared for her and the baby, too.

"Have you heard from Jonathan?" she asked.

Ty shook his head. "Not since I talked to him last Sunday. He'll be home next week."

And then maybe the house won't feel like an empty shell, he thought grimly. He could have come over and eaten with Shane and Tina every night, or he could have eaten with the ranch hands. After Monday night, he'd chosen to eat alone.

"How's the moving going?" Shane asked when Tina went back inside with strict orders to yell when she needed stuff brought out. He poured two glasses of iced tea and handed one to Ty.

"Okay."

"But?" Shane questioned, hearing the things Ty didn't say.

"But not as fast as I'd like."

"How's it working out with the female wrangler?"

"Venita does a good job. Actually, women seem better with the cattle than some of the men, but it's hard to keep them. They tend to get married and have babies.''

''Hmm.'' Shane turned the chicken pieces, poked them a couple of times with the fork and declared them done. He turned off the gas to the grill and moved the chicken to a platter on the warming shelf next to a loaf of sourdough bread.

''Hmm what?'' Ty asked, knowing there was more that his brother was thinking.

''You should think about a brother or sister for Jonathan. He confided to me that he wanted one a whole lot when he was last here. He needs someone his age on the ranch.'' His brother gave him a calculating glance.

Ty scowled at him. ''Is that why you sent Carly Lightfoot to be the cook's helper? Was she supposed to tempt me into married bliss again?''

''Why not?''

Tina leaned out the door of the sun room before he could tell his brother off with a few succinct words. ''Okay, you two, you can bring the rest of the stuff.''

Ty felt a surge of affection for her. She'd been good for the family, drawing him and

Jonathan into the circle of her and Shane's love, making them welcome. Tina and Shane worked together as a team. He'd thought to have that closeness with his wife.

It hadn't worked out that way. While Tina and Shane had been falling in love, his marriage had been falling apart.

He set his thoughts resolutely away from the past. Life was what it was. A person had to accept that.

He brought out platters of vegetables while Shane carried plates and silverware. The two men took their seats at the round patio table. The tiles beneath their feet gave off the heat from the sun while the evening air cooled rapidly.

"Have you been avoiding us?" Tina demanded, handing the chicken platter to Ty.

He had. Since Jonathan had been gone last summer and again for this vacation, the loneliness had closed in on him. He was glad for his brother and sister-in-law, but sometimes…well, their happiness got to him.

"Nah," he said. "I've been working."

They chatted and ate, then sat in the warm sun room until nine o'clock. He helped his brother clear the table before climbing in his pickup and driving home.

The house was dark. He'd forgotten to turn on any lights before leaving. As usual. He went into the study, flicked on a lamp and settled in his favorite chair. With the remote control, he turned the TV on to the news. He wanted the sound of a human voice in the house, even if it was an illusion.

"Now for the weather," a woman was saying. "What's in store for us over the weekend, Charlie?"

The news anchor had dark hair and eyes. Like Carly Lightfoot's. He'd heard Elena and Martha discussing Carly and the friend she was visiting for the weekend. They had questioned whether Carly really was going to visit a female friend.

He wondered, too.

The women liked her in spite of her continued friendship with Rodrigo. She was a good worker who didn't complain and didn't mind what she did. She liked to explore the ranch and seemed to enjoy living there—

He realized where that line of thought was taking him. He was not considering another marriage no matter what his son, brother and sister-in-law wanted or decided was best for him.

After the news, he flipped to the PBS station. A nature show depicting life in a far jungle was on. He'd seen it before.

His thoughts reverted to his newest hand. Lightfoot. An Indian name? With that hair and eyes, she could pass for Native American. He was as curious about her as Martha and the women.

It would be nice to have someone who liked ranch living, who didn't mind real work as opposed to planning a charity ball, who would love him and his son—

Damn Shane for putting ideas in his head. Neither of them knew a thing about the woman his brother had hired and sent to the ranch without a single reference. Except she'd responded to his kiss as if they were made for each other.

"You're awfully introspective."

Carly glanced at her friend and sighed. Isadora Chavez was an actress—beautiful, poised and with presence, as one critic had put it. Isa had been her best friend since high school.

The two friends sat in the dining room of the lodge at the Rogue Mountain Resort. They'd eaten breakfast and now lingered over coffee and the Sunday paper. Isa's teenage brother had spent the night with friends, so they were alone.

Carly put down the financial section of the paper and gazed into the distance. The view was wonderful. "Did you ever get the feeling you've bitten off more than you could chew?"

Isa laughed. "Only on opening night of every play and every night thereafter." She laid the comics on the table and poured them each another cup of coffee from the insulated carafe the waitress had left. "So tell me what you've bitten off," she invited. "Has it to do with this crazy idea of working on a ranch instead of resting?"

"Yes. No. Sort of."

"Hmm, profound, I see."

Carly made a face at her friend.

"So, what's happening?" Isa sipped her coffee and gazed at Carly with a worried frown.

"The work isn't the problem," Carly said glumly.

Isa's delicate winged brows, which Carly had always secretly envied, rose a fraction. "Oh?" she said.

"Well, it is, but not in that way." She sighed and gazed out at the mountains surrounding the long, rolling valley. A lone cloud loitered over the top of a nearby peak. Ski trails cut through the fir and pine trees on the steep slopes. The resort was prosperous and busy with hiking groups and nature lovers.

"For heaven's sake, will you tell me what's going on?"

"Did you ever hear of mad infatuation at first touch?"

"Ah." Isa laid a hand to her breast and quoted from Shakespeare, "'Whoever loved, that loved not at first...touch?'"

"Get that gleam out of your eye. I'm not in love. It's just that...whenever I see him, I have this insane desire to touch him...and have him touch me. It's a sort of primitive *lust*."

"Hmm."

"He feels it, too. It's baffling."

"Has he...did you...how serious is it?"

"Not that serious." Carly picked up her cup and hid behind it while she confessed. "We kissed once. But that was all," she added quickly. Isa looked relieved. She tended to worry about other people, probably because she'd had her dad and brother to take care of since she was ten or eleven. Her mother had died early. So had her father. She'd raised her brother alone for years.

"Isa, it was scary. I went all weak and shaky inside. I wanted him to keep kissing me." Carly gave her friend a puzzled, desperate look.

"Who is he? One of the cowboys?"

Carly shook her head. "Worse. Ty Macklin."

"Oh, Carly." Isa was all sympathy. "The Macklin men have a reputation for being hard and cynical."

"The oldest brother—the one who's the sheriff—is married now. He was very nice when I interviewed for the job."

"He has to be. He's a public figure. I've heard the other one has become harder since his divorce, a woman-hater."

Carly pictured the laughing man who teased

the other workers and who'd kissed her. She sighed. "Daydreaming about him is stupid. Nothing can come of it, but when he's around, I get all fluttery and dithery." She looked up, bemused. "That can't be love. Can it?"

"I don't know."

They fell silent. Carly felt bad because she'd probably called up painful memories for Isa with her silly tale about Ty and herself. Isa's fiancé had walked out when she'd refused to put her brother in a foster home four years ago.

Men. Who needed them?

"Well, it's almost noon." Isa stretched and began gathering her things from the chair and table. "It's time for me to head back to the condo. Do you stay in a bunkhouse at the ranch?"

"Actually, in a house with two other women. It's sparse, but nice. It reminds me of a camp I attended one summer. The aunt and uncle I was staying with wanted to go on a cruise, so they sent me to a neat place in the mountains. It was fun."

Isa folded the paper and slipped into her jacket. "Be careful," she said with a worried frown at her friend.

"I will. I never do anything rash."

After they said their farewells and Isa left, Carly lingered at the resort. It was the perfect place for a gift boutique, she realized, forcing her mind to practical considerations. She spent most of the day checking out the stores in the lodge, then stopped and bought a chicken dinner on the way to the ranch. She'd have a picnic by the river, she decided, while she gave serious thought to her future.

After parking her car beside the frame house, she took her supper and started off, walking east along an old orchard before cutting through to the river. On the grassy bank, she sat down to eat her meal in the solitude of late-afternoon sunshine while she made plans for her store.

The resort was the ideal location. She'd start checking on it right away. She nodded in satisfaction. Having a definite goal was good. It made her feel more settled, more secure. She yawned and scooted into a comfortable position. Her lashes drifted down.

Ty hung up the telephone in relief. Jonathan was booked to come home the following week.

He'd be glad to see his son. God, if he missed him this much during the few weeks he'd spent away from the ranch, what would he do when the kid went off to college or moved out on his own?

Probably become emotional and embarrass the boy to death. It was bad enough when a kid's mom broke down and cried in front of all his friends, but it was awful if his dad did it.

He managed a wry chuckle. Leaving the house, he stopped on the lawn and gazed over the lush, rolling pastures marching along the river and all the way to the mountains.

As he often did when alone, he walked the land, alert for fungus and diseases that could destroy the grass or the herd. He liked working with nature…or contending with it.

A late snow in the spring had delayed moving the cattle to higher pastures, and the grass had been overgrazed, but it had recovered okay. He'd left a lighter herd on it during the summer. October rains had replenished the fields. Now, with a late Indian summer, things were looking good.

With a satisfied nod, he continued his stroll.

When he came to the river, he watched its swift passage for a time, noting the drop in its level. Most of the snowpack had melted from the mountains weeks ago. Soon winter would build it up again for another year.

Another year.

Jonathan would go to regular school soon. He'd been sick a lot last year with colds. The doctors had suggested home tutoring for a few months. By next month, the boy would be caught up with his first-grade class, and the medical men thought he could try regular school again. Ty was a little hesitant. After nearly losing Jonathan, Ty wasn't taking any chances with his son.

Walking on, he rounded a gentle curve in the bank and stopped. For a long minute, he observed the woman sleeping by the gurgling water. Carly Lightfoot. Cook's helper. Temptress. Enigma. The few facts he knew about her didn't jibe. He walked over and sat on the grass, waiting for her to wake.

The first thing Carly saw when she opened her eyes was Ty Macklin, seated beside her, as still as a cat sitting beside a mouse hole in a field. She gasped and sat up.

''Sorry, I didn't mean to startle you,'' he said with a smile that was not exactly friendly but not exactly...well, she couldn't tell what it was exactly, just that it gave her a chill. ''I hope you don't mind my joining you?''

Her heart pounded wildly while she stared at the man who'd haunted her dreams for a week. Something about this encounter did not bode well. ''Not at all,'' she finally murmured.

He sat a couple of feet from her, his legs crossed Indian-fashion and his elbows resting on his thighs.

She noticed he toyed with a long blade of grass. His hands were big but elegant, the fingers long, with a smooth grace to their movements. They'd been gentle when he'd touched her. So had his kiss, even though it had started in anger.

But it had ended in something else— She stopped the inane thought, pulled her gaze from his hands and looked into his eyes.

He stared at her intently. She shifted uncomfortably, feeling as if he could see every libidinous notion in her head.

She couldn't figure out what had triggered this ridiculous attraction. During her years in the city, she'd been exposed to men who were handsome and successful without having a single flutter. So why was she having them now?

"How was your first week?" he asked.

"Fine." At his shrewd glance, she added, "Except for my arms, shoulders and legs aching at night. Other than that, it was a piece of cake."

Her confession drew a wry laugh from him. "When my father put me to work holding calves while they were branded, I thought my arms were going to fall off the first day. By the third, I wished they would."

She was skeptical of his childhood. "Did you actually work the ranch?"

He nodded.

"How old were you?"

"Twelve when I started really working. I was big for my age," he said when she frowned at this information. "Before that, I pulled the water wagon for a couple of years. I was always glad when school started so I could quit."

Curious about his past, she started questioning him. "Were you a good student?"

His grin was quick and dazzling. "Yes. Dad's punishment for low grades was to make us boys work longer and harder. When I figured that out, my grades improved by leaps and bounds."

Carly had to smile at his droll expression. If she hadn't sworn off men, she would have fallen for this one. But having talked it over with Isa, she had everything under control.

She noticed he was watching her, observing her features as intently as an artist would study a painting. A tiny thrill went through her. She couldn't tell if it was fear or desire.

He reminded her of a wild creature, sleek muscled and ready to spring. She sensed a restlessness in him, a hunger for a part of life that was missing from his. She saw it in his eyes.

At that same instant, she knew what it was, for she felt it, too. Loneliness. And passion.

It sizzled between them. The air suddenly seemed too hot to inhale, and her mouth went as dry as cactus fuzz.

"Yet, in spite of your childhood, you took

over the ranch.'' Her voice came out husky, sexy.

''I like growing things.''

The quiet statement, the deep sense of satisfaction in his voice and in his gaze as he glanced at the acres of pastures, told her he did. The knowledge did strange things to her heart.

''The workers are happy here,'' she ventured. ''Do you bribe Elena and Martha to sing your praises?''

''I've never had to pay a woman for anything.''

His direct look challenged her to make something of his swift innuendo. She started to make a remark about his ex-wife, but stopped herself in time. His past was none of her business.

''Then perhaps you've had things too easy since you became an adult,'' she suggested, an understated challenge in the words.

One dark eyebrow rose fractionally, and a flicker of emotion whipped through his eyes and was gone. ''Maybe,'' he agreed. ''Why do I have the feeling that's about to change?''

She shrugged. Why, indeed? Because there

was something that pulsed to life each time they met, something she wanted to reach for, the same way she wanted to touch him.

His eyes locked with hers. Again the air sizzled between them. She couldn't be imagining it. It was too strong, too earthy and elemental, not to be real. He felt it, too.

Or was he faking it? Was this his manner with women, to make them think they, and they alone, wakened some slumbering passion in him? She'd been fooled by a man's ardor once before.

''Where are you from?'' he asked suddenly.

''Chicago.''

''Do your parents live there?''

''They're dead. I lived with an aunt when I was growing up in a small town in western Illinois.''

''What did you do before you came here?''

His questions came rapid-fire, like an inquisition. The suspicion in his eyes was clear, but what did he suspect her of?

''If this is an interview, you're too late. I've already been hired.'' She gave her hair a toss over her shoulder.

''There's something here that doesn't fit.''

He narrowed his eyes as he thought it over. "I'll figure it out."

Puzzled, she tried to figure him out. "Let me know when you do," she finally said.

"You look familiar," he told her.

She shook her head. "I haven't been in this area before."

"You remind me of the cover girl on the farm magazine I got last week. Did you ever do any modeling?"

"No."

Shaking her head firmly, she saw his gaze go to her hair. It was loose, tumbling down her back and probably full of tangles from her nap.

"You have the looks for it." A cynical hardness coated the compliment. "A certain wholesomeness that's popular now."

"Hmm, maybe I should try it, except I'd have to go to New York to be a model, wouldn't I?" She grimaced to show her dislike of that idea.

"Doesn't the city appeal to you?"

"No."

The conversation had entered a different sphere as he probed into her personal life in the way she'd done with his. The tension inside her increased. His expression was unreadable, but she felt certain he wasn't asking questions out of mere curiosity.

"What does?"

The undertone in the softly spoken inquiry touched a chord in her and set it to vibrating, but she'd learned to handle sexual innuendo years ago. She smiled lazily and shrugged. "Um, I don't think I'm going to answer that."

"Then I'll have to find out on my own." There was no mistaking his intention of doing just that. He looked her over, as if assessing every quirk of character, every trait and flaw she possessed. "Excitement? Danger, perhaps," he mused aloud. "Some people thrive on it."

"The adrenaline rush," she murmured. "No, thanks. I like my life quiet and sane."

She'd watched some friends bungee jump. They became addicted to the thrill of it. She wasn't one of them.

"Is that why you're here?" His expression had hardened ever so slightly. "For the quiet?"

She lifted her head and gave him a cool glance, then watched the river again. "Yes."

The only danger was losing her head over him.

"You've seemed nervous each time I've seen you. Is it only when I'm around?"

She pressed a hand to her breast, looked at him and gave a great sigh. "Be still, my heart," she murmured, her glance openly mocking his vanity.

His ears turned pink. Well, at least he had the grace to realize how conceited his question had sounded. When he grinned, her heart turned over. "I shake when I'm around you," he said softly, suggestively, sexily.

"Hmm, maybe that's what makes me nervous. I'm wary in the presence of a known predator."

He smiled sardonically. "Don't worry. I choose my quarry carefully...and I always give warning before I pounce."

She rose, aware of his gaze sliding over her before flicking back to her face, aware that if she baited him past a certain point, she would have to live with the consequences. Yet she wasn't afraid of him. Of herself, yes. Of him, no.

"But I don't," she said, and walked off.

Her heart was pounding fiercely. Behind her, she heard him laugh, a deep, husky chuckle that made her want to rush to him and not look back.

Chapter Four

The house was dark when Ty entered by the back door. He flicked on a light in the kitchen. The place was gleaming and smelled of lemon cleanser. Martha, who looked after the house, did a good job. Other than that one concession to need, he and Jonathan bached it on their own.

He wondered if his son missed a woman's touch in the house and realized that he did. His mother had been a wonderful woman, mediating her husband's tendency to harshness with a gentle hand. The ranch had been her favorite locale, and she'd made their home a warm and welcoming place.

His former wife had remodeled the kitchen before they'd built a new home closer to town and her friends. She'd liked to cook and had done it well. During the first year of marriage, he'd been eager to come home at the end of the day.

He frowned, then sighed. Somehow, it had all gone wrong. She'd grown dissatisfied with their life, which revolved around the weather and the seasons, the ranch and the cattle, never mind that the money for the vacations and shopping trips she'd wanted came from those very things.

He cursed silently and put the memories aside. He'd gotten Jonathan out of the deal. His son had been worth the large divorce settlement and the pain of knowing it wasn't him but his name and money that his wife had wanted. He'd be damned glad when the boy came home.

He peered into the refrigerator and got out the makings of a sandwich. When his son was home, they ate in the ranch kitchen. Then he pored over the endless paperwork while Jonathan did his homework. They had a good life.

The silence of the house mocked that observation.

Life was just the way he wanted it, he reminded himself. No women to clutter it up. If he felt the need for company, he could visit Shane and Tina, Martha and Buck or other friends.

He piled ham and cheese on whole-wheat bread, added some carrot sticks and pickles to the plate, grabbed a beer and went into the family room to eat. He flicked on the TV to catch the weather before the news went off, then left it on to fill the silence until it was time for bed.

Yeah, he had a life. Only it was empty as hell with no one in the house but him.

Carly stretched, then turned back to the kitchen. Elena was stirring a pot big enough to boil a missionary and humming along with a song on the radio. They were making soup for supper.

The ten-o'clock news came on. Carly listened to an account of tornadoes touching down in Texas, followed by a story of a trip by the president and first lady to California for a meeting with foreign dignitaries.

Just then, a short but broadly built man came in. She grimaced as Pete Hodkin helped himself to coffee and pastries set out on a side table. Glancing over her shoulder, she saw his eyes on Elena, taking in her friend's shapely backside while the woman reached into the upper cabinets.

A feeling of distaste invaded her. Hodkin had a slimy way of sizing up a person, as if considering his personal gain while he looked them over.

He called out a greeting, which she and Elena returned without further conversation. He turned his gaze on her. "Martha says you're doing all right."

A tingle of pride rushed through her. She nodded her head in a modest gesture. The man seemed to be waiting for something more from her. "Yes, well, I like it here."

It was Wednesday of her second week. The other hands were at ease with her, and she found they were opening up to her more each day. But, out of the dozen people who worked on the place, she didn't like this one man.

Ty strode in, grabbed a cup of coffee and a doughnut before sitting across from Hodkin. The men talked about the horses and the problems with keeping them healthy. Carly listened more to the sound of Ty's voice than the actual words.

"That cracked hoof won't heal," Hodkin said. "We're going to have to put the gray down."

The meaning penetrated her dreamy haze. She looked up from the potato she was paring. "My grandfather had a way to fix that," she broke in, remembering the Indian remedy. "Make a rawhide shoe for the horse, put it on while damp and let it shrink-fit to the hoof. That will keep it clean and sealed."

Carly wiped the sweat off her forehead with her sleeve and went back to work. The crew ate potatoes every day. Hadn't they ever heard of rice or pasta?

The kitchen was warm and humid. Clouds covered the sky, adding to the high humidity. October usually cooled off, with chilly nights and mornings and temperate afternoons, old Martha had told her. November would be the start of the rainy season.

Realizing the silence, she glanced around. Elena, Hodkin and Ty were watching her. She returned their stares, puzzled by the sudden attention.

"Your grandfather raised horses?" Ty asked.

"Yes."

"In Illinois?"

"No. He was Hopi. It was on the reservation."

She saw more questions in his eyes, but he turned to the remuda hand. "Let's try it."

Hodkin shrugged. "Sure." The two men left.

"You didn't tell me your grandfather was Indian," Elena said. "Did you live with him?"

Carly reminisced about her visits to the ranch in Arizona that she'd loved while she and Elena sat on the porch and shelled peas. She could grow to love it here, too, she realized.

Through the leaves of a live oak, she saw Hodkin come out of the stable and talk to the young woman who worked as a wrangler. She didn't look more than eighteen—a girl, really.

Carly watched Hodkin chuck the girl under

the chin, apparently teasing her about something. Although the youngster smiled, Carly could tell she was uncomfortable in his presence. Seeing his face when he turned partly toward her, she realized he knew it, too.

And didn't give a damn. Lust was clearly in his thoughts. The feelings of the girl didn't matter. Carly's distaste for the man returned, stronger this time. She would give him a piece of her mind....

"Stay out of it," Elena said, reading her intent.

"But he's bothering her—"

"She needs the job. She helps support her family."

"But no one should have to put up with someone like him in order to make a living. It isn't right."

"What do you know of right, you with your fine car and your education?"

Carly stared at her friend, dumbfounded. "My education?" she repeated stupidly.

"Do you think it doesn't show?" Elena's expression softened into an exasperated smile. "You ask lots of questions, yet you don't know how or when you will be paid. You drive an almost new car, yet you don't need to work on Saturday for money to make the payments. The others think you're hiding out here on the ranch for some reason…from parents or a lover, perhaps.''

Carly was startled at how close they'd come to the truth. ''The women have been talking about me?''

''Of course. We talk about everyone. What else is there to do when we're through with our work?''

''Sit and gossip,'' Carly concluded. Seeing Elena's warm, teasing smile, she relaxed.

''So, are you running from cruel parents or a lover?''

''An ex-fiancé who decided he'd made a terrible mistake and wants to start over.''

''Do you?''

''Horrors, no. I was lucky to get rid of the jerk.''

The sounds of male laughter floated to them on the afternoon breeze. Ty was in the vicinity. Her entire body went on alert. It was odd, the things he could make her feel just by laughing.

''I'm looking for a place to settle,'' she said

slowly. "A place that's mine." She shook her head, helpless to explain.

"You need a mate and babies." Elena fingered the long strand of baroque beads around her neck, a handmade gift from her girls.

"Oh, yeah, right," Carly scoffed, laughing at the idea.

"It is nature. Men burn and women yearn, yes?" Elena gave her a sly grin, then nodded toward the stable. "He will come."

He did.

Strolling across the stable yard, Ty approached the porch and stood watching them work without speaking. The two women were silent, too. Carly observed him warily from the corner of her eye. He studied her as he had last Sunday, as if trying to figure out what made her tick.

The thought made her nervous, causing her to drop a pea. It landed at his feet. "Ah, manna from heaven," he murmured, scooping it up. He ate the tender vegetable.

Elena laughed. Carly could imagine those strong white teeth taking a playful nip at her. The cook was right—she did yearn.

"Have you seen Hodkin?" he asked.

"Yes, he was outside a few minutes ago. He went that-a-way." Carly pointed in the direction the man had gone.

"We're going to try your grandfather's treatment." Ty walked off, covering the ground at a rapid pace. Carly breathed a sigh of thanks. Like the approaching storm, she had a feeling things were coming to a climax.

Friday afternoon, Ty paced the worn carpet in the gate area. Jonathan's plane had touched down ten minutes ago. Most of the passengers had gotten off, but not Jonathan. He scowled at a flight attendant when the man walked past.

"There are a few more passengers to debark," he said.

"I'm waiting for my son."

"Jonathan?" At Ty's nod, the man grinned. "He's a neat kid. The captain let him in the cockpit and offered to let him fly the plane. Jonathan took the copilot's chair, cool as could be, and told the captain he could bring it in. You know something, I think he could've."

Ty laughed when the attendant did. An unbearable knot of love for his son settled in his throat. God, he'd missed the boy.

Another flight attendant, a woman this time, left the plane. She had a small boy with her, and they were chatting easily.

Jonathan looked up. "Dad," he yelled. He flung himself headlong up the narrow ramp and into his father's arms. "Guess what? I got to fly the plane, the whole thing, all by myself."

"He did a great job," the woman confirmed. She paused beside them. "It's obvious who you are—Jonathan has told us quite a bit about you—but may I see your identification?"

Ty showed her his driver's license. She checked the name against a piece of paper and nodded approvingly. The glance she gave him was warm and more than a little interested.

He thought of asking her if she wanted to join them for a cup of coffee, but before the thought had more than formed, another face appeared in his mind—one with dark, flashing eyes and a sharp little chin with a stubborn tilt.

"Thanks for taking care of Jonathan," he said sincerely.

"Dad, have you ever been in the cockpit?" Jonathan asked, eager to tell of his adventure.

"No, tell me about it." Ty waved goodbye

to the attendant and went with his son to collect the luggage. He wondered if he was passing up an opportunity for a great relationship. A temporary one. There was no room for a permanent woman in his life.

He tried to blank Carly out of his mind. Without success.

At nine, with Jonathan settled in and asleep in his room, Ty was no nearer to forcing Carly from his thoughts than he'd been all week. He hadn't seen much of her the past few days. Was she avoiding him or he avoiding her?

He wanted to find out who she was and why she was working there. He was more than halfway convinced she had some ulterior motive for being there. Looking for a rich husband?

That was hard to believe. Ranchers were not known for having a lot of loose change. Besides, she didn't try to attract him. And she was a darned hard worker, hardly the attitude of a social climber or fortune hunter. Maybe...

He stomped into his room, flung off his clothes and climbed into bed. He was a fool to let a female haunt his life this way. The busy season would be over in another couple of weeks, then she'd be gone.

Good riddance.

A burning sensation inside belied that sentiment. Oh, hell. He tossed back the covers and yanked on jeans, shirt and a jacket. Ramming his feet into sneakers, he went out to walk until he was tired enough to sleep. It took a long time.

Carly yawned and laid her head against the rock she used as a backrest. The sun cast long shadows over the landscape. Saturday afternoon was her favorite time on the ranch. Most of the hands were in town, and she had the place to herself.

Her mind stubbornly strayed to her boss. She'd seen him arrive at his home with his son yesterday. The boy had been talking a mile a minute, and Ty had listened with grave interest and an occasional smile. A good father.

Men burn and women yearn.

Did she yearn for home and hearth, for a mate and children as Elena insisted? Were hormones and nature's ruthless survival-of-the-species instinct the cause of all the flutters she got when he came around and when she thought of him?

He seemed to feel something equally intense toward her. She wasn't blind to the male-female attraction. But it was all so strange. To want and be wanted like that.

Before now, other than her parents and Aunt Essie—she wasn't counting the jerk—no one had ever wanted her very much. Self-pity? she mocked. No, the cold, hard truth. She'd faced it years ago.

Hormones she could handle. Love was the scary thing. It worried her. She didn't want to do anything silly like fall in love. She had her future to think about.

''Well, what have we here?''

Carly stiffened at the rough, masculine tone. Then she realized it was some distance from her. She sat up cautiously and looked around. The old orchard that separated her favorite place from the ranch road was no longer deserted. Two figures, almost hidden by the trees, had invaded her space.

She recognized Hodkin at once. The other person was smaller and partially hidden by his thick bulk. His companion answered, the words indistinct, but the voice clear. The cowgirl. Venita was her name.

"You trying to get away from me?" Hodkin asked, and gave a nasty laugh that had Carly curling her hands in anger. He knew he had the girl trapped alone here in the woods. Or so he thought.

If he tried anything, he'd have more than one enraged female to deal with. She picked up a chunky rock and rose to her feet in one smooth, silent motion.

"Don't play coy with me," Hodkin growled. He had the girl by the shoulders. She wasn't fighting, but she had her face turned to the side and was clearly distressed. Only a brute would keep on when he was so obviously not wanted.

"No, please, I must go in," Venita said.

He caught her hair in one hand and brought his mouth down on the girl's.

"Let her go," Carly ordered, so furious she wanted to bash him right that instant. She walked over to them, stopping about four feet from the pair.

Hodkin raised his head and gave her a withering glare. "Mind your own business."

Carly shook her head. "When a person says no, it means no."

"Nobody said anything to *you,* so get lost."

"Yeah, well, I'm funny about some things. I don't like to see a woman forced to endure some slime-bag because he thinks he's the world's greatest lover."

"Why, you…" Hodkin snarled.

He moved swiftly, but Carly was prepared. She sidestepped when he flung Venita at her. Grabbing the girl's arm, Carly steadied the younger woman, careful not to take her eyes off Hodkin, who'd noticed the rock in her hand.

"Think you're pretty big with that rock, don't you? You need taking down a peg or two, sister, and I'm gonna do it for you."

When he lunged, Carly would have moved aside again, but Venita clutched her arm in fear, stopping any movement. Carly, realizing she wasn't going to be able to dodge, swung her head to the side and rocked back on her heels.

She caught a glancing blow from his fist and tasted the warm saltiness of blood in her mouth as her bottom lip was trapped between her teeth and his knuckles.

"First blood to you," she said politely, as

if they were engaged in a formal duel of ancient times. She then clobbered him with the rock.

Unfortunately, his head was thick. The blow merely made him angrier.

"Get back," she said to Venita, jerking her arm from the girl's hold and dropping the rock. She needed both hands free and room to move in order to perform the self-defense tactics she'd learned in karate class.

Hodkin swung at her again. This time, he barely tapped her. She grinned at him, a sure-fire way to disarm an enemy—make him think you're really enjoying the fight. That little trick made most people think twice about attacking.

She crouched into a defensive posture, intending to toss him over her shoulder on his next strike.

"Hodkin!"

The bellow of rage froze the three contestants. Ty stalked out of the shadows. Without a pause, he moved in on Hodkin, his broad fist hitting the other man's jaw with a bone-shattering crack.

Hodkin's eyes rolled back, and his knees buckled.

"Out like the proverbial light," Carly said in satisfaction when he folded and fell to the ground. She grinned at Ty.

He gave her a look that would have melted a steel spike, then he turned to Venita, who stood to the side, trembling in every limb. "You all right?"

She nodded.

"Go on to your room," he ordered, his voice quite gentle considering that he looked ready to kill.

She cast one more terrified glance at the man on the ground, then headed for the path back to the women's quarters.

Carly gingerly touched her throbbing lip. It felt twice its normal size. Her finger came away bloody.

Ty grasped her wrist. "Come on," he orderly grimly.

"What about him?" she asked, looking over her shoulder at Hodkin, who was groggily rising to an elbow and peering around as if looking for the truck that had run him down.

"Be off the place within the hour," he said to the man, "or I'll escort you off. You understand?"

Hodkin gave them a mean-eyed glare, but nodded his head.

Ty ushered her through the woods at a headlong pace after one more fiery glance at the downed villain.

Carly quickened her pace to keep up. "He's a terrible person. No wonder Venita was scared of him."

Ty snorted. "You could take some lessons in that department. What the hell do you mean taking him on like that? He would have chewed you up and spit you out as confetti in another ten seconds."

"But you saved me," she argued. Now that the incident was over, she found it highly amusing. She batted her lashes at Ty when he favored her with another glare.

"Don't push your luck," he snarled. "I'm still thinking of stripping your hide inch by inch and throwing what's left in the river."

"You and whose army?" she demanded, feeling in high good humor now that the danger was past.

He ignored her. They reached the road. He led her across it and into his home. There, he paused in the kitchen, which looked like a pic-

ture from *Architectural Digest,* and grabbed a
paper towel and a couple of ice cubes.

He wrapped the cubes in the towel and
handed them to her before guiding her up four
steps, down a short hall and into a bedroom.
From there, they entered the largest bathroom
she'd ever seen.

"Wow, who does this belong to, the
queen?"

"Keep that ice on your lip," he ordered. He
rummaged in the medicine cabinet. He came
up with a tube of ointment. He perused the
instructions, grunted in satisfaction, screwed
off the top and squeezed a small amount onto
a finger. "Look here."

She removed the ice pack and raised her
face to his. He rubbed the cream into her lip.
It felt better almost at once.

"Okay, put the ice back on."

"Yes, sir." She pressed the ice pack to her
lip.

"Don't get smart. I've still got a lot of
adrenaline pumping through my veins," he
warned her.

She thought she must have quite a bit of it
running around inside her, too. She felt light-

headed, but extremely lucid. Everything—him, her, the room—glowed with an incandescence that was strange and wonderful.

The terrible anger flashed into his eyes again. ''When he hit you...'' He stopped, and she saw his jaw muscles work when he clamped his teeth together.

Lifting her free hand, she touched his sleeve. Through the material, she felt the heat radiating from him. She rested her hand on him and felt the tension in his arm.

''Don't,'' he said, looking harried and angry and perplexed all at the same time.

She couldn't help herself. Slowly, she ran her hand up his arm and over his shoulder. She trailed her fingers across his collarbone until she reached the strong brown column of his neck. She found the pulse there, beating strong and steady.

Laying her hand flat against his chest, she soaked up the warmth. Closing her eyes, she savored the strength in his body, ready to be used at his command, and marveled at the fact that he'd used it for her.

''How did you know I needed you?'' she

asked. Her voice seemed to come from a long way off.

"I know where you go when you want to be alone."

"I see." He knew her habits much better than she knew his. And knowing she was alone down by the river, had he followed her for reasons of his own?

"You always spend time by the river during your free time. I was out walking when I saw Hodkin's truck on the side of the road. I didn't know if he'd...bother you."

She heard the pause as he chose his words and knew he'd been deeply concerned for her. "Not me. It was Venita he wanted. He's spoken to her a couple of times this week, so I knew he was after her."

"And you went to her rescue."

"Mm-hmm." She didn't want to talk. Actually, she wanted him to kiss her. A sort of sleepy languor washed over her, and she swayed against him.

He uttered a low curse, then picked her up. Carrying her into the bedroom, he laid her on the huge bed, removed her shoes and sat beside her. After turning on the bedside lamp, he frowned at her as if he didn't quite know what to do next.

The thought occurred to her that probably he had never had a woman in his bed that he wasn't intent on making love to. This had to be a new experience.

All sorts of fantasies danced through her head as she mulled over the things they could do. If they were lovers.

He removed the paper towel she still held to her lip. With his thumb, he pulled her lower lip down until he could see the injury. He leaned forward to inspect it.

"The bleeding has stopped," he reported. "I don't think you need stitches. I would advise against eating anything hot and spicy for a few days."

She smiled, carefully because her lip hurt when she moved it, at his wry advice. She wondered if he fell into the category of "hot and spicy."

Curiosity got the better of her. She licked her tongue across his thumb and tasted the slightly salty tang of his skin.

He drew his hand back, startled. When she lifted her gaze to his face, his expression was stern and unreadable. She waited, not sure what he would do.

"You're just asking for trouble, aren't you?" he said after an eternity of heartbeats.

She shook her head, then changed her mind and nodded yes.

He bit out an expletive. "You get to me faster than any woman I've ever met."

"Is that good or bad?" she dared to ask.

The room was filled with soft shadows as the sky darkened into deep twilight. The cone of light from the lamp enclosed them in its golden hue. The atmosphere was private and intimate and very, very nice.

"Oh, it would be good." He laughed, the sound soft but harsh with cynicism. His glance raked boldly over her, effectively changing the subject to one deeply personal between them.

"I know." It was a simple answer to a simple truth. Simple? she mused. Yes, simple... and complicated and dangerous.

Heat flared in his eyes, and she knew he'd thought of her this way, of the two of them alone in the privacy of his bedroom, more than once. She'd done the same. Passion had sizzled between them from the moment of that first contact. It hadn't let up.

Stealing a peek at him through her lashes, she knew she had to be careful. He was still high on the surprising fury that had erupted when he'd come to her rescue. She wanted more than an adrenaline rush, more than passion, between them.

As sudden as a spring shower, she knew she was in danger of falling in love with Ty. Panic washed through her, then subsided. She'd learned long ago not to fight what life dished out. To do so was an exercise in futility. But falling in love...no way.

"You had better watch what you say. You're alone with me in my bedroom," he reminded her, his tone cool, his eyes hot. "Aren't you worried about your virtue?"

"I'd never worry with you."

That brought him up short. He stared at her, as if trying to figure her out. She held his gaze.

He raised one eyebrow, giving her a quizzical look. "Are you inviting me to make love to you?"

It was with a sense of pure elation that she

realized she wanted that very much. "Not now. Not this way."

"What way?" he challenged. "I'm willing to try anything within reason." He gave her a knowing look.

She cursed the women who had come before her, those who had made him hard and skeptical and cautious.

"I wonder if you know…" he began.

"Know what?" she asked, feeling a hazy languor spread over her like a warm blanket. It was really too hard to think.

"What your eyes are saying." His gaze skimmed her lips, down her body, then returned to her eyes. "Do you?"

She laid her hand on his chest, unable to resist touching him when he was so close. He felt nice to touch. His eyes darkened as she let her hand trail down to rest on his thigh, palm up. He laid his hand over hers.

"Yes," she whispered. "I know."

This wasn't like her. She was cautious and levelheaded. She was ambitious and career-driven. There was no place in her life for a man.

"Anything we share, it's for the moment only," he said with savage honesty.

She felt the pain of rejection, as if he'd promised her the moon and taken it back.

He leaned over her, his mouth very close to hers. "You didn't like that. Did you expect oaths of undying love?"

"Would you give them?"

"No. Don't expect anything of me but this." His lips met hers on the last word.

Any answer she might have made was forgotten in the wonder of his touch. He glided over her lips, lingering here and there, with the softest of caresses. His gentleness was her undoing. Fury she could have resisted, but this…no.

"Give me your mouth," he coaxed.

She opened her lips. A tiny groan escaped him before his tongue slipped inside and flicked against hers. His arm stole behind her, pulling her close until her breasts were pressed to his chest. She felt his breathing quicken.

She wasn't prepared for the sparks that shot away down inside her, nor for the wildfires they set off in secret places in her body. When he slipped one hand into her hair, she wrapped her arms around him and held on.

It came as a surprise, this gentle flow of passion, not at all like the kiss in the twilight last week. She gave a little cry of delight. It felt so good to be held this way.

Just when she thought she might drown in ecstasy, he lifted his head. He was breathing hard, as hard as she was.

"You'd take me right here, right now," he said.

"Yes."

"Why?"

She wasn't prepared to answer that.

"What's in it for you?" he demanded.

"Nothing."

"Nothing but a pleasant toss in the blankets?" He shook his head. "A woman like you, you'd expect more than that."

"A woman like me?"

He watched her, his eyes so dark with emotion they looked black in the lamp light. When the telephone rang, he continued to study her while he picked it up. To her surprise, his expression softened when he heard who was on the line. "Good," he said. "Yeah, you can walk by yourself. I'll meet you halfway.'' He said goodbye and hung up.

She started to swing her legs off the bed when he stood.

''Stay here,'' he ordered. ''Jonathan had dinner with Martha and Buck. He's on his way home. I need to put him to bed, then I want to talk to you.''

''What about?'' She felt dizzy as she sat up. Those couple of blows had been more damaging than she'd thought. She lay against the pillows and waited for the wooziness to pass.

''You know the answer to that.''

The quiet accusation in his voice caused the wild heat to run over her again, starting from some fire deep inside and running to her skin, bringing a flush with it.

He touched her cheek, a gesture at once seductive and oddly tender. ''You seem so totally without subterfuge. I wonder…''

''What?''

''What you'd take from a man.'' He paused at the door. ''And what you'd give.''

He left her there on his bed, wondering the same things.

Chapter Five

Carly must have dozed off. She sat up, startled, when she heard a child's voice in the hall.

"It was really neat, Dad. Do you think I could try it?"

"We'll see, son." The standard parental delaying tactic in answer to a child's eagerness for life.

She smiled, then winced at the painful pull on her lip.

"It's for free, and Mike's mom said she'd bring me home."

"Sounds like you have it all worked out," Ty said with wry amusement.

"So can I? Please?"

"I guess so. But you have to listen and do everything the coach tells you. Learning to rope is hard work."

"Right. I'll be really careful."

Carly crept off the comfortable bed and padded over to the door. Ty and a youngster about six stopped on the marble steps.

"Who're you?" the boy asked with friendly curiosity.

"Carly Lightfoot. Are you Jonathan?"

"Yes. Are you visiting my dad?" He looked beyond her to the bedroom, then returned his gaze to her. "Say, are you my new mom?"

She was astounded by the question. For once in her life, she was completely without words.

"No, she isn't," Ty said.

The boy looked disappointed. "Your hair is really long," he went on. "All the way down your back. It's pretty."

"Thank you."

"Are you going to stay with us awhile?"

Carly wondered how many other women had "stayed" with them.

"No," Ty broke in decisively. "She was hurt, and I had to treat the injury."

"Oh. Where did you get hurt?" Jonathan asked Carly, at once interested in this new fact.

His eyes, she noted, were the same sky blue as his father's, but his hair was light blond rather than tawny.

"My lip." She bent down so he could see and touched the sore spot to show him.

He studied it for a few seconds. "It doesn't look too bad," he assured her. "Hardly swollen at all."

"It's time for your bath," Ty reminded the boy.

"You can come talk to me," Jonathan invited. "My friend and I are going to take rodeo lessons and learn how to ride and rope a bull. Have you been to the rodeo? We're going to have one at school for Halloween. Neat, huh?"

"It sounds super. I remember reading about it in the paper," Carly said, falling into step beside the talkative boy.

Jonathan chatted happily about learning to rope. Like his father, he hadn't a shy bone in his body.

Ty wasn't contributing much to the conversation. However, he didn't seem to mind his son talking to her.

The boy's bedroom was a child's delight. The bed was part of a gym-and-storage set. A desk was tucked into the structure, too. There were lots of nooks and crannies in the room, all filled with books and games and fun things to do and learn.

"This is very nice," she said, noticing how it all went together for optimum storage, leaving a broad play area in the middle of the room.

"My dad and I designed it," Jonathan said proudly. "Then we built it, well, him mostly, but I helped."

Carly looked at Ty. His expression mocked her surprise at his abilities. She'd learned that he liked growing things and experimenting with new types of cattle and working with nature during her days at the ranch. Now she knew he also liked building things. And that he cared very much for his son.

The love was evident in every movement, every inflection of his voice, as he started the shower and laid out pajamas, then reminded Jonathan to put his clothes in the hamper and that the water was running. The man had a soft spot, after all.

"We'll have a story after my shower," Jonathan told her. "You can listen to it if you want to. Can't she, Dad?"

Ty hesitated, then nodded. "Sure."

She realized he didn't like her being there, listening to their intimate family life. Well, too bad. She hadn't asked to come. After all, he was the one who'd dragged her to his home and insisted on doctoring her.

Her lips burned as she recalled that strange kiss. By some instinct, she knew that he'd wanted to kiss her passionately and without restraint, but he hadn't. He'd been careful.

It gave her a strange feeling to know he was, for all his bruskness and cowboy toughness, a considerate person.

Jonathan went into the bathroom and closed the door. In a minute, she heard him singing in the shower. She turned her gaze upon Ty, knowing whom the boy got the habit from.

He shrugged in an offhand manner. "In the shower, everyone sounds like Caruso."

His embarrassment was endearing. The idea of him singing in the shower, as well as other images that thought invoked, caused her breath to catch in her throat. Inside, she went all nervous and fluttery as usual.

She watched while he turned back the covers on the high bed with its railing all around like a log fence. He put away a couple of toy trucks and straightened the room.

The sounds of the shower stopped. In another minute, Jonathan came out of the steamy bathroom dressed in cotton pajamas.

There was something very sweet about a child who was clean and ready for bed. This one had a curious vulnerability about him. His trust in the world was absolute. As hers had been long ago.

"Come sit on the bench with me and Dad," he invited.

She glanced at Ty and got his slight nod before advancing to the wide, padded bench built under the window. Jonathan sat in the middle, between her and his father, and picked up the book he'd selected. He handed it to Ty and settled against a wedged-shaped cushion. Ty opened the book.

His baritone voice, with the attractive grittiness in it, rumbled pleasantly in the room as he read the adventure story. He made the tale

come alive as he and Jonathan became en-
grossed in the lives of a pioneer family.

It seemed to her that the mere sound of Ty's
voice held the night at bay, and that all the
good things in life were safely encircled and
contained here in this room by that voice. It
was a sound to lull angels to sleep.

Her lashes drooped heavily against her
cheeks. She could hardly hold her head up. She
shifted more comfortably against the cushion
and forced her eyes open. Looking at Ty and
his son caused an ache in her heart.

She wondered about the woman who had
been in their lives and had left. What a fool
she'd been to give them up.

When the story was over, Ty tucked Jonathan into bed. The boy kissed his father, then
looked expectantly at her. She went over and
received a kiss on the cheek and a hug. It made
her feel funny inside, as if her skin were suddenly too tight for her body.

"I told Dad I wanted him to get us a new
mom. I have my real mom in New York, but
we need one for here, too. I like you." He
touched her hair, which was cascading down
over her shoulders. "You're pretty."

"Thank you," she said, feeling very humble. The gift of trust and friendship was a precious thing.

She walked out while Ty finished saying good-night to his son and discussed a project for the next day. She lingered at the door. Watching them, a strange notion leapt into her mind and refused to budge. She wondered what it would be like to be the woman in their lives…the one they needed on a daily basis.

Ty came into the kitchen right after the coffee finished heating. She poured two mugs and took them to the breakfast bar. "Your home is lovely," she said.

The kitchen had a beige counter that looked like smooth sand but was of man-made material. The floor was textured vinyl, which she'd first thought was green marble. Some of the white cabinets had glass doors. Behind them, she could see crystal bowls and glasses that looked expensive.

A pattern in the beige-and-green curtains had been duplicated in the wallpaper that covered one wall and was continued down the hall. Green and white were the dominant colors in the house.

"It should be. We paid some decorator enough to retire in style by the time she finished with it."

Carly smiled. "A typical male attitude. You'd have probably been satisfied to slap some paint around and call it quits."

"What would you have done?"

"With this room?" she asked, stalling as she thought of sharing a house with him. It sounded like fun to pore over books and ideas together.

He nodded, coming over and sitting on one of the leather bar stools on the other side of the counter from where she stood.

"I like it as it is. I'd add some plants, maybe an herb garden in the greenhouse window." She nodded to the window that jutted out from the wall.

"That's what it's for. My ex-wife liked to use fresh seasoning when she cooked." He took a drink of the coffee she'd found in the pot and reheated, then peered into the cup as if wondering if he could trust her not to poison him or something.

"Was she a gourmet cook?" Carly asked, feeling very put out with him because of his ex-wife's cooking ability. She was such a lousy cook. When she invited her friends over for dinner, they always came early and took over the kitchen themselves.

"Yes."

His expression didn't invite further discussion, but she was intrigued by his former marriage and what it had been like. "The way to a man's heart and all that," she murmured, lifting the coffee mug and taking a drink. She nearly choked.

He raised one sardonic eyebrow and took another drink of the sludge that was supposed to be coffee. "Yes. She was good in the kitchen. Too bad we couldn't stand each other any place else."

Carly wanted to ask about the bedroom, but even her boldness didn't extend that far.

"There, too," he murmured with a wicked leer.

Heat flooded her face. "What?"

"You were wondering if she was good in the bedroom. She was. To a point."

She stared at him, her heart beating wildly, knowing she didn't want to hear any more.

"The point being that she gave or withheld her favors as she saw fit in order to get her way. After a while, a man finds he can live without them."

"Most women can't separate their emotional needs from their physical ones the way most men seem able to do."

He pounced on that statement. "Can you?"

"I...we're not talking about me."

All at once, he was close to her, leaning across the breakfast bar until he was in her face. He caught a handful of her hair, which still tumbled around her like a tattered curtain. She thought he was going to kiss her.

"Perhaps it's time we did. Why are you here?" he demanded in a seductive murmur that almost took her off guard.

"What do you mean?"

"You're obviously not cut out for life in a ranch kitchen. Is this some kind of adventure for you? Are you doing research for a book or an article, perhaps an exposé on the Macklin family?"

"No. None of the above," she answered truthfully.

"What, then?"

She saw he wouldn't be put off. "I wanted to get away, to go to a place I wasn't known where I could…think over my life."

"Ah," he mocked. "The great search for the true self."

"Not at all. I wanted to get away from a jerk." She leaned forward and gave him a meaningful stare to indicate he might be included in the designation if he pushed too hard.

He returned her glare for a few seconds, then the corners of his mouth curved upward in a sardonic grin. "You must have been pretty desperate. Who was he?"

"My ex-fiancé. He thought, after trying and failing to get part of everything I owned by claiming to be a de facto business partner, he could step back into my life."

She knew her expression had gone "mulish," as Aunt Essie would have said. She felt mulish when she thought of how gullible she'd been. She wanted to kick the jerk out of her life...or over the moon, whichever was furthest.

"You've just had a humorous idea," Ty remarked.

Carly nearly spilled her coffee in surprise at his insight. "How did you know that?"

"Your mouth indents at the corners when you mentally smile."

"Oh. Well, yes, I was thinking I'd like to kick him over the moon or someplace equally far."

"So what did you have that he wanted?"

"A tiny gift boutique. Actually, three of them, in hotels in Chicago. I called them the Powder Box I, II and III."

He snapped his fingers. "That's it. I saw you on TV, a show about women in business who made it without outside help. What happened to the stores?"

"I sold them. I wanted a new life free of memories. I'm trying to decide where I want to settle. I'm checking into the resort near Ashland. It has a good tourist business, and I have a friend who lives there. If that doesn't work out, I was happy with my grandfather in Arizona. I might go there."

He ignored the last part. "Ah, yes, the friend who caused so much speculation among the women. Elena said it was a woman."

She nodded, not taking her eyes from him. He was a more volatile person than his teasing had indicated when she'd first met him. And more complex, she decided, recalling his manner with his son. An interesting, complicated human being.

"So why did you come to the ranch as a hired hand?"

"Maybe I'm looking for a rich husband." She gave him a once-over, then grinned at his irritated expression.

"That you can take to the cleaners?" His laugh was cynical. "You've come to the wrong place, sweetheart. This sucker has been there, done that."

She poured out part of her coffee and added water to dilute the strong brew. "All right, I did have a reason," she confessed. "My ex-fiancé was calling daily. My friend had her own problems. When I saw the ad in the paper, I realized it would provide a nice, quiet hideaway. Besides, it sounded like fun."

That sounded like the most idiotic excuse in the world.

"The great American myth of the West." He pushed his cup toward her. "Add some water to this mud," he requested.

She did and handed the cup back. He took a drink while he considered. "All right," he finally said. "As long as you behave yourself, you can stay. One more incident and you're out of here."

"Behave," she echoed. "I haven't done a darned thing but wash dishes and peel potatoes since I came to the blasted ranch. Hodkin wasn't after *me*."

"Yeah, but you stepped in and wounded his dignity. The man could be a serious enemy. His truck was gone when I went to meet Jonathan. I forgot to have Buck put a tail on him to see where he went." He flicked her a glance that singed her insides.

Carly knew quite well why he'd forgotten. Those few minutes in the bedroom had driven every thought from her head, too. "He wouldn't dare hurt me." She gave a disdainful sniff. "Like most bullies, he's probably a coward, too."

"Right. That's why he'd watch and wait for a chance to get you alone. He also has friends who might be willing to take part in the fun."

"Yes."

His eyes narrowed. "You've already thought of that. Any clues as to who?"

She shook her head. "He was with two men at Smitty's a couple of weeks ago. I saw him when I went through town."

"Would you recognize them if you saw them again?"

"No."

He drank the diluted coffee while studying her with his cool, calculating gaze. "I wonder if you're telling the truth. You didn't hesitate to use the outcome of your episode with Hodkin to your advantage."

That statement baffled her. "What do you mean?"

"You're in my home," he said. "My son has seen you in my bedroom and thinks you're going to be his new mom—"

"That was your doing, not mine," she said hotly. "I don't have designs on your virtue, if that's what you're insinuating. You dragged me into your home and bedroom, playing the

Good Samaritan until we were alone, then you kissed me when my guard was down.''

''You didn't exactly fight me off.''

She was furious that he would remind her of her conduct. ''That was not a gentlemanly thing to say. I was hurt and dazed, probably in shock. A lot you cared—''

He dared to laugh. ''Tell me another one before that one gets cold,'' he scoffed.

''I would really like to hit you,'' she growled at him. A pain flashed through her head, and she became aware of a headache. ''You made my head hurt,'' she accused, pressing against her temples.

''Yeah, well, you make me hurt in a couple of places, too. My head is just one of them.'' He stood and paced the imitation-marble floor irritably.

After a tense, silent two minutes, he gave her an amused perusal, once more in control of his temper. She wasn't going to confess that he made her ache, too.

''Are you working with the police?'' he asked suddenly.

She gave him a blank stare.

He correctly read her confusion. "I can see you're not."

"Is the sheriff investigating Hodkin? Perhaps I can talk Venita into pressing charges."

Ty gave her an exasperated frown. "Stay out of it. There's been some thieving on both sides of the state line the last few months. A couple of ranchers have been hurt. Fortunately, no one's been killed. Yet. My brother is working with the local sheriff to try to break the case."

Carly mulled this over. She was willing to bet Hodkin was in on any scams. "Elena said Hodkin had only been working here for about six months."

"What's going on in that busy little brain of yours?" Ty glared into her eyes as if he could read her every thought.

"Nothing. I have to get back to the house. Elena has probably returned and is wondering where I am."

"What is she, your watchdog?"

"My friend. That's something you should cultivate more of, instead of cows," she suggested sweetly. She stood, eased around him and headed for the door. She didn't make it.

His big hand closed over her shoulder, forcing her to face him. "Not so fast. I'm not sure it's safe. Until I know Hodkin is out of the vicinity, I want you where I can keep an eye on you."

"That's ridiculous."

"The women think you're a runaway heiress. Hodkin might get ideas along the same lines."

"An heiress! Why would they think that?"

"Designer jeans. A fancy car. You figure it out."

She sighed. "I thought I was doing so well."

"You are," he said on a quieter note. "You're a good worker."

"Well…thanks." She was inordinately pleased at the compliment. "It's hard, but kind of fun, being with the other women and talking to them."

"Not to mention Rodrigo," Ty said dryly.

"He's cute, but not my type."

"Hmm," Ty said.

She realized how close they were. His eyes bored into hers. The yearning grew inside her until she had only one thought—she wanted to be in his arms again. His gaze was open to her all at once. She saw hunger and need and desire. For her. Just for her.

"Damn you," he said.

She thought the two words were the loveliest ones she'd ever heard. From some deep well of understanding, she knew exactly what he meant. They were a recognition of the feelings between them, feelings that couldn't be suppressed.

When he swept her against him, she didn't resist. It was an impossibility. The need was too great.

She realized she'd never been in love before. Whatever she'd felt in the past had been a girl's crush compared to the welter of emotion she experienced with this man. She wanted to entwine herself in him until neither could tell where the other started or ended. It scared her to want someone this much.

His mouth sought hers. She felt a shudder run through him, but he was gentle when he touched her lips. He examined her injury with his tongue, running over her swollen lip and the teeth marks inside it so very carefully.

When he left her mouth, she gave a little cry

of frustration. He swooped down and pressed his mouth to her neck, laving her with hot, hot kisses that increased in ardor with each one.

She ran her fingers into his tawny locks and clutched him to her, her heart beating so wildly she feared it would never find its rhythm again. His hands ran down her back and over her hips. With perfect ease, he lifted her to fit against his tall, strong frame.

Whimpers of need filled her. She could never have imagined feeling this way, not in a hundred years. It was magic.

When he placed her on the counter of the breakfast bar, she opened her thighs and felt him step close, their bodies touching intimately. The hard ridge of his desire pressed against her. She felt the softening within herself as her body made ready to receive him. She longed to feel him inside....

"Dear heavens," she whispered, shocked by the force of this terrifying longing.

His mouth ravaged her throat, her face. "You go soft in my arms," he murmured, more to himself than her. "And I go up in smoke when I touch you."

"I know. I know," she crooned incoherently.

He lifted his head, his eyes glittering like melted glass. "Yeah. It isn't something a man can hide."

"Neither can I," she retorted, feeling a reprimand in his confession. "It's...*unreal.*"

"It's that, all right," he agreed with a grimness that stung. He stepped away from her, running a hand through his hair in a resentful gesture. "I have no place for this in my life."

"You think I do?" She leapt off the counter to the floor and grimaced when the bounce made the blood pound in her lip.

"I'll get your shoes." Whirling, he walked out.

She gripped the counter with both hands, willing the faint trembling to leave her body. If she had any sense, she'd leave. Except she didn't want to. She wanted to stay and play out this strange drama to the very end.

"Here." Ty entered the kitchen and thrust her sneakers at her. He gave the holes in the shoes a sardonic glance.

She leaned against the cabinets to pull the comfortable old shoes on. "I have a hard time throwing out old things. They seem a part of me,'' she explained defensively.

He merely cocked one eyebrow. ''What's next on your agenda?'' he demanded. He folded his arms across his chest, his expression as remote as the face of the man in the moon.

''I don't know,'' she said truthfully.

''I want you out of here.''

''You want me to quit?''

''Yes.''

''No.''

His eyes went as dark as a thundercloud.

''You have no reason to get rid of me. I didn't do anything wrong. I want to finish out the month.''

He drew in a deep breath and let it out in a loud sigh. ''You'd probably find another job nearby just to drive me crazy.''

She grinned, knowing he was relenting. ''I would. I'm thinking of opening a boutique at the ski resort. Working here gives me a chance to scout around without any complications—''

His snort of scornful laughter stopped her protest.

''Well, except for us…for this.'' She indicated the passion that bloomed between them at any opportune moment. Like whenever they saw each other.

"All right," he said, coming to a decision. "Don't try any of your feminine wiles on me or anyone else. I may lose my head when I touch you, but I am capable of rational thought otherwise. Give me any trouble, and I'll have you off the place faster than you can spit."

"You won't know I'm around." She knew she was in the clear. He was going to let her stay. What was more troubling was the fact that she wanted to. She wasn't ready to walk away from him. "So, what are we going to do about Hodkin?"

"You're not going to do anything. I'll take care of him."

"How?"

"None of your business."

"Maybe I'll get it out of you at a weak moment," she suggested wickedly, then nearly choked on laughter at the look on his face.

He stepped closer, forcing her to move back or have to crane her neck to peer up at him. "I just may let you try it," he muttered, a definite threat in his manner.

"Promises, promises," she quipped gaily, then sprang back out of his reach.

She knew she was teasing a tiger, but she'd discovered early in life that a smart mouth could cover a lot of uncertainty, especially when cousins taunted an unwanted relative. Around Ty Macklin, she was anything but confident.

"You do like to live dangerously." He moved with lightning speed. Before she could do more than grasp the fact, he had her in his arms. "Now what are you going to do?"

"Shout for help?"

He shook his head. "That isn't your style." He moved his hands restlessly in her hair, entangling the long strands in his fingers as he slid them upward along her back.

She tried to hold his gaze to prove to him she wasn't afraid, but her lashes kept dragging her eyelids downward. She knew she should fight him, but the will to do so wasn't there. She sighed, a shuddery sound of indecision.

His breath flowed softly over her lips as he bent toward her. "You confuse the hell out of me, too. I want you, but I know better than to get involved. You're like a rose patch, with pretty flowers on the surface but with long, dangerous thorns hidden in those bright trappings to ensnare the unwary.''

''I'm not trying to ensnare anyone,'' she denied, coming out of the sensual trance he induced.

He released her abruptly. ''Good. Because it won't work on me. I've been led down that path. Believe me, once was enough.''

''I'm not like your wife.'' She was insulted that he'd compare the two.

''Ex-wife,'' he corrected. He walked over and held open the kitchen door. ''Let's go.''

She knew it was useless to protest his walking her to the house. No one was on the place, not on Saturday night. Even Elena had gone to town this time.

However, when they arrived at the edge of the trees, Ty stopped and let her go on by herself. It was a good thing. A lone figure sat on the stoop to the women's quarters. Carly recognized Elena's familiar form in the deepening shades of twilight.

''You're home early,'' she said to her friend, crossing the small clearing.

Elena rose and came to her. Laying a finger

across her lips to indicate silence, her friend drew her back into the shadow of the oak trees. Carly felt a stir of foreboding at this secretive behavior. It wasn't her usual manner.

"You must go away from here," Elena said in a near-whisper.

"Why?" Carly asked.

"There was talk tonight at Smitty's. Hodkin and a couple of his friends were drinking. They got to talking about what should be done about a woman who didn't mind her own business. You should leave here."

"She is," a masculine voice spoke from the dark. Ty stalked from the shadows in the woods and joined them.

"I'm not afraid of him. I've had self-defense courses," she protested. "I'll not be run off by a bully."

Elena gave an exasperated snort and turned to Ty. "You made it worse by taking her to your house."

He stuck his hands on his hips in a belligerent pose. "She was hurt. Surely the word has spread about Hodkin hitting her."

"Yes, but when someone is hurt, you normally take them to the office and fix them up, not to your home…your bedroom," she added with a soft giggle.

"My bedroom, how did anyone know—?"

"The light can be seen from here. Often the women have joked about joining you there."

He gave a groan of disgust. "Nothing is private around this damned place. I suppose everyone in three states knows how many women I've had in the house since my divorce."

"None," Elena promptly stated. "Martha is worried about you. She says it is time you found a real wife and made some babies."

"Hasn't she noticed that I have a son?" he inquired with a great deal of sarcasm.

"But that was not the true marriage. It will come—"

"I hope not," he broke in. "My problem right now is what to do with this woman." He peered at Carly through the gloom.

She realized the attraction between her and Ty had made the situation worse. She could be a source of danger. If something happened to him or his son because of her…

The decision was made in an instant. She'd have to leave. "You don't have to worry about me. I'll be out of here in ten minutes. Will that be soon enough?'' She headed for the house.

Behind her, she heard Elena say something and laugh again.

True to her word, she was ready to leave in ten minutes. She went outside with her luggage. Elena and Ty were waiting.

She held out her hand. ''It's been fun.''

Elena took her hand, but didn't shake it. Instead, she pulled Carly into her arms and gave her a hug. ''You're a good worker. I'll give you a recommendation any time you need one.''

Carly squeezed her friend and reluctantly let her go. ''You've been wonderful to me. Thanks for all your help.''

Ty picked up the suitcase she'd dropped in the grass during the farewell. ''If the goodbyes are over, let's go.''

''So anxious to get rid of me? Gee, it didn't seem that way up in your bedroom.''

Elena covered her mouth, but not before a fresh wave of laughter broke out.

''Just keep it up,'' Ty warned, looking close to the end of his rope. He started for the road and her car. She fell into step behind him after waving once more to Elena.

Carly felt a teensy bit guilty for taunting him about their wild passion. That was something he wouldn't have to worry about, that she'd trap him into marriage or anything.

She, too, had been burned. She hadn't once considered marriage to him.

Well, maybe once…

Chapter Six

Ty stopped by the office to sign the payroll checks on Thursday. He noticed the date. November 1. He looked over the accounts before pulling the check ledger toward him. He'd had more than a dozen people working the ranch the past month.

This week there were two fewer hands than last week. Carly Lightfoot's name wasn't on any of the checks. She'd left last Saturday, and he hadn't seen her since.

She might as well be present, though. She interrupted his sleep with nightly visits in his dreams. Memories of the few kisses they'd exchanged lingered in the back of his mind like a melody he couldn't tune out.

Thinking of her mouth made him think of the way she'd responded to his kisses. They'd been wild, those kisses. Each time he and Carly met, there was an instant, mindless explosion of passion between them. It scared the hell out of him.

Oddly, she hadn't tried to deny it, nor had she used it to get anything for herself the way some women did. The attraction had surprised her as much as it had him, but she hadn't pretended it wasn't there.

An honest woman. Who'd have thought it?

As if he were watching a private TV screen, her image flashed into his mind. She had a way of looking directly at a person, her eyes so candid and trusting a person had to believe what she was saying.

As they said in the communications business, she had a high credibility rating. Or maybe he just wanted to believe the way she gazed at him. As if he were wonderful.

Yeah. God's gift and all that. He gave a snort, mocking his own vulnerability to a pretty face and a trusting gaze.

He knew better. Women were subtle creatures. He'd seen more than one in action. For instance, he'd had a mean stepmother get her hooks into his dad before he died. She'd tried to make off with the family farm. Fortunately, the judge had put a crimp in her plans when the case went to court. Still, she'd gotten a large chunk of money, which they'd needed for new equipment.

And then there had been his ex-wife. She'd cleaned out his pockets as neatly as any con artist on the police roster, smiling innocently all the while.

Carly hadn't pretended to be an innocent. She hadn't acted coy or skittish. No, she'd just gazed at him as if she'd been struck by stardust each time he'd touched her. It had been unnerving to look into eyes that looked back at him in wonder.

His body reacted the way it always did to thoughts of her, coming to attention with a hot ache stabbing through him.

Frowning, he scratched his name on the checks, making them official, and ignored his physical demands. When he finished, he stacked the checks neatly on the desk for the new secretary to hand out the next afternoon.

"Hi, Ty. Are these ready?"

Martha's granddaughter bounced into his office, the morning mail in her hand. She placed it in the In basket on his desk, glanced at the checks to see if they were signed, then picked them up to lock them in the safe for the night.

She gave him a glance that would have had his glands in an uproar if he'd been about twenty instead of thirty-five. Alys was a flirt, but a good-natured one. She laughed at his scowls when she got too bold about his personal life.

"No big date this weekend, huh?" she blatantly asked, standing on one red, three-inch-high heel and wrapping the other foot around her ankle while she leaned against the desk. She'd have been insulted if she knew he thought of her more as a kid playing dress-up than as an adult.

"Now, what makes you think that?" he asked, wary of her nosy questions and inquisitive black eyes.

"You're not smiling. A man who's looking

forward to getting a little…entertainment over the weekend should look happy.''

He idly took in her lush, womanly figure. Martha was right to be worried. Alys was ripe for adventure. Her figure was full and inviting. And she knew how to use it to advantage.

Carly, on the other hand, was a small woman. Her breast had fit neatly into his palm.…

He cursed silently and pushed the image from his mind. ''What?'' he said, realizing she'd said something else.

The carmine lips went into a pout. ''Never mind. You never hear a word I say, anyway.''

He chuckled. ''Maybe you should learn to talk less and say more,'' he suggested.

''That doesn't make any sense.''

''Yes, it does. Think about it.''

A sly look came into her twinkling black eyes. ''Maybe you liked what that other woman was saying when she was here. What's the matter? Isn't she coming back? Is that why you've been so grouchy all week?''

His fuse burned down while he counted to ten, then twenty. He stood, drawing himself to his full six-one height, which was about a foot taller than she was. "You're the secretary, not my social director," he reminded her far more gently than he felt. "You'd better lock those checks in the safe and get back to work."

Her cheeks turned red, and tears of mortification filled her eyes at his reprimand. He felt like Simon Legree. Not that she didn't deserve a scold. She was much too bold, but still, he didn't like hurting her feelings. "You've done a good job since you've been here," he added. He picked up his hat, jammed it on his head and walked out, pretending not to see her grateful smile. "I'll be over at Shane's for lunch if anyone needs me."

He strolled across the stable yard, taking the long way to the house. The pastures were green and lush after two days of rain early in the week. He breathed a deep sigh of relief. It looked as if it would be a good year.

Shane had the news on when he arrived at his brother's house. Two trays were set up, sandwiches already on them. A salad, along with a plate of fruit, cheese and cookies, accompanied the meal.

"Where's Tina?" Ty asked, taking the easy chair opposite his brother.

"She's having lunch with Genny up at the resort. Can you pick her up in a couple of hours? I was supposed to go get her at two. However, I got a call from the office and have to be in court this afternoon."

"Sure."

"Jonathan glad to be home?"

"Yeah. He missed his pony."

Shane chuckled. "Is he still excited about starting school with the other kids and riding the bus?"

"He thinks it's wonderful, but it's only the first week."

"Twelve years to go, then college. Poor kid."

Ty chuckled with his brother and thought of the long days, months and years of schooling kids went through before they could call their lives their own.

"I want to ask you a question," Shane mumbled around a big bite of turkey sandwich.

"Shoot," Ty invited, trying to ignore a dark-haired, dark-eyed woman on TV as she laughed at something the weatherman was saying. Her coloring reminded him of Carly.

Shane swallowed and wiped the mayo from the corners of his mouth. "What happened to the woman I sent down to help Elena?"

"She left." Ty tried to speak casually. "There was some trouble." Such as those moments in his bedroom. Big trouble.

A twinkle came into Shane's eyes. "Oh, like that, is it?" he questioned softly.

Heat gathered in Ty's ears. "Nothing *like that*," he snapped. He tersely related the incident with the wrangler. "She packed up and took off. I haven't seen her since."

"Hmm." Shane ate his sandwich while they listened to the weather report. When it was over, he spoke again. "I was thinking of hiring her to put the ranch records on the computer. Martha's girl doesn't know how to load and set up the system."

"What makes you think Carly would?"

"When she applied for cook's helper, she saw the financial package the county uses. She said she'd put it on her computer, and it was the best she'd ever used."

Ty mulled this news over. "Then you knew

she'd had her own business before you sent her to the ranch?''

''Um, yes.'' Shane dropped out of the conversation to listen to a news report of an accident on the interstate highway.

Ty heaved a deep sigh. With his son insisting on going to school—''Now, Dad. I want to go now''—and without Carly's disturbing presence, not to mention the cowboys who'd moved on to other ranches or the rodeos, the ranch felt deserted these days.

He finished his meal and settled back with a tall glass of iced tea. ''Why did you hire her?'' he asked after a long drink. ''She was a bit overqualified for a cook's helper, wasn't she?''

Shane wiped his mouth and tossed his napkin on the tray. ''Nah. She said she was a terrible cook.'' He laughed outright at the grimace Ty shot him. ''If looks could kill, I'd have to arrest you for attempted murder,'' he drawled in warning. ''Actually, since she seems footloose, I thought I'd see if she wanted an undercover job with the department—''

''Like hell you will.'' Ty pushed his chair

back so hard, it tipped on two legs, then settled to the floor with a thunk. ''Leave her out of your plans.''

''Well, if you feel that strongly about it.'' Shane shrugged. ''I'll see if I can catch my man and tell him not to contact her.''

''You know where she lives?''

''Yeah. Do you?''

Ty faced the challenge in his brother's eyes. ''Yeah,'' he said, and dared Shane to make something of it. ''I followed her when she left the ranch. To make sure Hodkin wasn't on her tail.''

''Hmm.'' The news went off. Shane clicked the remote control, and the screen went dark, the dark-haired reporter disappearing.

Ty experienced a flicker of emotion, a sort of strange pain, as if his own life had been turned off. Well, it had been for two years, and it had been damned peaceful. Carly had brought him back to the living with a kiss.

Blasted woman.

She'd invaded his thoughts and his every dream so that he didn't sleep well at night. Instead, he lay in bed and wondered what she was doing. Several times he'd walked half the night so that he could fall into an exhausted slumber…and he still dreamed of her. Stupid, really stupid.

A man who didn't learn from his past mistakes deserved what he got. He pushed the TV tray away and stood. "I've got to go. I'll pick Tina up. Two o'clock, right?"

"Yeah. Thanks, brother. I'll do something for you sometime."

"Just keep your wife happy," he advised sardonically. "Else I'll make a play for her."

"Sure you will…and you'll live another ten seconds after you do." Shane, too, stood. He stretched lazily, obviously not at all worried about his wife's or his brother's loyalty.

"Thanks for lunch. See you later." Ty strode out of the comfortable old Victorian that had been built in 1920 after the original farmhouse had burned down. For a moment, he felt the sharp bite of envy.

He thought about it as he walked to the truck. He didn't actually envy his brother his happiness. He just wished he had a dollop of it for his own. If things had been different…

Well, no use crying over spilled milk and all that. He'd made a bad choice before, choosing a woman because of her looks and her smile. He wouldn't be foolish again. Jonathan would have to wait a long time before they found a live-in mom. If they ever did.

Ty was going to know everything there was to know about the next woman he let in his life. One thing for sure—she wouldn't be somebody's ex-fiancée looking for a hideout from her boyfriend.

He shopped for the items on the ranch list, checked the time and headed for the mountain resort that looked out over the valley.

The Rogue Mountain Resort was pleasingly busy for a ski area in November, Carly observed. The owner had successfully developed it into an all-season resort. From the number of people with knapsacks and sturdy backpacks strapped over their shoulders, it was a popular place. She liked what she saw.

She climbed out of her car and went into the huge stone structure. Bill Johnson, a man in his early forties with an easy manner about him, met her in the lobby. Dressed in khaki pants and a blue work shirt, he had the look of a woodsman about him rather than that of building/vendor manager.

He greeted her and commented on the weather. "Hot today for the first of November, isn't it?"

Carly nodded and agreed it was. A part of her was still amazed at the date. The weeks had flown by like dandelion fluff in a gale. Because she'd been at peace for the first time in months, she realized. At the ranch, she'd been happy.

"About this time every year I begin to wonder if fall will ever come," he pursued the topic while leading her up the steps. "The temperature soared into the high eighties in the valley yesterday. Of course, it was cooler here on the mountain."

Mr. Johnson guided her toward the entrance to the restaurant on the second floor. She suppressed the questions she had while she took in every aspect of the place.

The resort was bustling. It had a year-round program of hiking, camping and nature-watching, as well as skiing. There was a lively conference-and-convention trade, too.

More and more, she thought it was perfect

for her business. The manager had agreed when she called him about her plan.

They were given a table for two in a window-enclosed alcove. The view was magnificent. Vistas of rugged mountains and green valleys delighted the eye in every direction. She breathed deeply as if taking the essence of beauty into her, then glanced around.

It was late, and the dining room was almost empty. The tables near them were unoccupied.

"What kind of bribe did you have to pay for this table?"

"I have connections," he answered her quip. When he chuckled, his voice was deep, the kind the bass singer in a quartet would have. "That's the boss over there. He told me to impress you."

A warm feeling of welcome flowed over her as she accepted a menu from the hostess. She watched the owner of the resort cast a proprietary glance over the restaurant as he went by. She'd spoken to him by phone twice the previous week.

"The salmon in the pastry crust is great," her companion advised. "So are the vegetable kabobs."

"The salmon, I think. Since this is on your budget and not mine, I can splurge."

When the waitress returned, they were ready to order. As soon as they were alone again, he leaned toward her. "I want to know exactly what your requirements are for the boutique, what traffic you need to sustain the business and what you expect as part of the deal."

She smiled, at ease in a business situation. "First, I have some questions of my own. There's no need in wasting our time if we don't mesh. I'm looking for a lease arrangement, not a partnership. I handle only my own stock, do my own ordering and have the final decision on location."

"The sheriff said you were sharp. He wasn't kidding." The manager chuckled.

After a surprised second, she did, too. What did the sheriff have to do with anything? He didn't know a thing about her.

Except her work history, of course. She'd told the truth on her application for the ranch job. Ty's older brother had accepted her explanation about looking for a place to relocate without visible doubts. Maybe he'd investigated her background.

The question was—why would he?

Bill sat back in his chair. ''Looks like we have company,'' he murmured in a low tone.

A male figure loomed beside them. ''What are you doing here?'' Ty Macklin demanded in a deep growl.

Carly started to tell him it was none of his business when she realized he wasn't speaking to her.

''Having lunch,'' Bill responded easily.

''I can see that,'' Ty snarled without glancing at her. ''She's out of this, you hear me?''

''If you have a problem, perhaps you should see the owner,'' she suggested. There, that sounded cool and in control. Her heart was pounding, though.

''The only problem I have is you.'' Ty gave her a hard glance. ''I talked to Shane at lunch. I'm not letting you do this.'' He turned on the manager. ''Stay away from her.''

Johnson tensed as if personally challenged. ''She's over twenty-one. I believe that gives her the right to make her own decisions on what she wants to do.''

Carly glanced from one to the other. Ty was furious. She could tell by the sweep of red up his neck. Johnson didn't look the type to back down from a fight. His arms were as muscular as Ty's, and she knew Ty lifted calves and bales of hay as easily as a soda bottle.

"No, she can't," Ty stated. He grinned.

She groaned at the feral gleam in his usually cool blue eyes and the challenge in that mocking smile. "I will do what I damned well please," she stated with haughty dignity.

Pushing her chair back, she rose, intending to march out and not return until he left. She'd gone no more than a couple of feet when a big hand settled on her arm. Ty walked out with her, his hold on her elbow propelling her along at his carpet-eating speed.

She looked back at Johnson.

He waved. "See you later," he called to her.

Giving him a nod over her shoulder, she faced forward and concentrated on keeping up with the man who seemed intent on getting her out of the place as fast as possible.

"My lunch," she said, digging in her heels outside the front door. "You're making me miss my lunch. Salmon in a pastry crust."

Ty released her arm. He gestured toward a couple of old-fashioned rocking chairs on the side porch. No one was around at the present moment. "Sit down. I want to talk to you."

She took a chair. "What?" she prodded when he didn't speak for a moment.

"Shane told me his man was going to ask you to help with a case they're working on. I want you to stay out of it. Undercover work is dangerous, too dangerous for a woman."

She hadn't the foggiest idea what he was talking about. She told him so.

"Weren't you two talking about an undercover job with the sheriff's department?" He nodded his tawny head toward the lodge and the manager they'd left at the table.

She stuck her chin in the air. "What if I am? You have no say in it."

A heavy frown settled on his brow. "Hodkin may be involved with the rash of burglaries in the area. If he caught you snooping around, he'd...you could be seriously hurt. If you need a job, the one at the ranch is open."

"Cook's helper?" She couldn't believe she'd heard right.

His lips thinned with annoyance. "No, the one setting up the ranch records in the computer. Shane said you were familiar with the financial program.''

''Oh. Well, yes, I am. However, I have another plan. That's why I was talking to the vendor manager here at the resort.''

''The vendor manager,'' Ty repeated as if he'd never heard the term. ''Wasn't he an undercover cop?''

''No.'' She explained her plans to open a shop in the resort.

Ty stood, his face as dark as a thundercloud over Rogue Mountain. ''That rat brother of mine. I'll get him for this.''

His muttered words made no sense.

''And you can't stop me,'' she finished, keeping her tone quiet.

His gaze flicked to her and bored holes right to the back of her skull. She held her ground. ''You're right,'' he said at last, smiling. ''You're a big girl. You can do whatever you want.''

''I can't figure you out. First, you don't want me at the ranch and you tell me to leave. Next, you offer me a job because you think I'm going to work for the sheriff. Does any of that make sense?'' she complained.

"Only in a certain context," he said ominously. He stood. "I have things to do. I can't sit around here talking all day. You'd better go back upstairs."

The wind wafted his after-shave lotion over her. She breathed it in greedily. Through the confusion of the moment, she realized he'd been concerned about her. It made her go soft toward him.

He sucked in a sharp breath. "Don't do that," he growled.

"What?"

"Smile like that, look at me like that."

"Why?"

"Because it makes me think things I shouldn't…like how it felt to kiss you and hold you. Then that makes me think of other things I'd like to do besides kiss."

"Such as?" she asked softly.

"Don't play games, Carly Lightfoot. You might come out the loser, and, believe me, that's no place you'd want to be."

"There doesn't always have to be a loser," she told him, wondering how the subject had become personal between them.

For a second, a haunted look appeared in his

eyes. He stared off into the distance. "But there always is."

It came to her that this man, as big and tough as he seemed, had his own areas of vulnerability. His son was one. Could she be another? She longed to hold him, to comfort him.

"Ty," she whispered. She reached out and touched his cheek. He didn't draw away. His gaze came back to her. For a long time, they stood that way, each gazing into the other's eyes, questions rampant between them.

"You could make me want...too many things," he muttered hoarsely, springing out of her reach. He stood by the porch railing. "Things I'd forgotten existed."

"Like what?"

"Truth, honor, loyalty, all that stuff." He'd become cynical again. "Then I remember you were living a lie the entire time you were at the ranch."

"I told you why I was there. It was the truth."

"But what about the other things...the things between us?"

"Kissing me outside the women's quarters, interfering with Hodkin, taking me to your bedroom, the kisses we shared there, those things weren't my fault. Not entirely.''

He heaved a deep breath. ''You're right. I'm sorry.''

His apology stunned her into silence.

He slanted her an amused glance. ''Now I know two ways to shut you up,'' he murmured, a tantalizing gleam in his eyes. ''Come on. Your lunch has probably arrived.''

He escorted her back to the restaurant. Johnson looked them over, then went on with his salad. After seating her across from the manager, Ty tipped his head to them and started to leave. At that moment, two women walked into the restaurant. They came to the table.

''Ty, I didn't know you were coming here for lunch. I could have ridden home with you,'' Tina Macklin said.

''You are. Shane asked me to pick you up. He had to go to court this afternoon.''

She accepted the change of plans graciously. ''Do you know Genny Barrett?''

''We've met,'' Ty said, and greeted her.

The other woman spoke up. ''Hello, Ty.'' She smiled at Carly. ''Are you our new proprietress?''

"If we can work out the details. I like your place." Carly turned from the resort owner's wife and spoke to Ty's sister-in-law. Tina Macklin, the sheriff's wife, was in the last stages of pregnancy. She looked healthy and happy.

Genny issued an invitation that included the group. "We're giving a reception for the new theater group that will be opening here at the resort next week. I hope you two will come. You'll get to meet the cast, as well as the playwright."

Carly realized Genny was issuing the invitation to them as a couple. As if they were dating. Her gaze flew to Ty's.

He gave her his usual sardonic smile, one corner of his mouth tilting up slightly higher than the other, lending his expression a definitely mocking edge.

Carly looked into his eyes and smiled disarmingly. His smile was replaced by a frown. She glanced away to find Bill Johnson watching the byplay between them with interest. A silent sigh escaped her. She'd have to watch herself around the building manager. The man saw too darned much.

Bill smiled as if he'd read her thoughts and wanted to reassure her that her private life was her own. She was grateful.

"Ready to go?" Ty asked, speaking to his sister-in-law.

Tina looked surprised at his abrupt question. She and Genny had been discussing the reception and the play. The proceeds were to go to the building fund for a new theater. "Yes, of course. I'll talk to you later, Genny." She said goodbye to Carly and Bill.

Carly watched as Ty cupped Tina's elbow and escorted her from the room. Genny Barrett said her farewells and left.

"Alone at last," Johnson murmured, amusement in his tone.

She gave him a rueful grimace. "Where were we?"

"I think we'd come to an agreement on the amount of the lease for the square footage of space you want and that you want it directly across from the restaurant. Is that right?"

She nodded.

"Then I think we've got a deal."

He stuck out his hand. Surprised, she shook on it.

Chapter Seven

Carly signed the lease for the new gift shop the following week. With her advice, Johnson directed the work crew in preparing the cozy alcove. The electrical wiring had to be added, and a gate, a metal one that rolled up like an awning, had to be installed to protect her goods when she wasn't in.

She commissioned the sign for the shop. The Cricket Cage was the name she chose. This new store would be nothing like the old ones in Chicago. A new place, a new name. She was pleased.

Now she had one more idea. For it, she needed Ty's help.

After checking that everything was going well at the resort, she dressed carefully and drove down to the ranch. First, she had to see about her merchandise, then she needed a place to live closer to the resort.

Her heart beat faster when she turned off the county road onto the ranch driveway. She parked in the shade of the oak tree at the side of the house. Her space, as she'd come to think of it during the time she'd worked in the kitchen.

The house had a deserted air. No one answered the bell. She waited another minute, then went to the office to look for Ty.

He was in. She spotted him as soon as she stepped inside. The door to his office was ajar, and she could see him through the narrow opening, talking on the telephone and riffling through some papers. He selected one and handed it to a young woman.

His secretary? Something awfully close to jealousy curled around her insides. The secretary came into the main room.

"May I help you?" she asked. She laid the paper on a desk and faced Carly.

The young female, hardly more than a girl,

was lovely in an overblown way. Her skirt was too tight and too short for office attire, her makeup too bright. Her lipstick matched the red, spike-heeled sandals she wore. Earrings dusted her shoulders with each move of her head. But she was pretty.

"I need to speak to Ty," Carly said, hiding the odd irritation she felt with the younger woman.

"Your name, please?"

"Carly Lightfoot."

"Oh, I read about you in the paper. You're opening a shop up at the ski resort, aren't you?" The girl's attitude changed in the blink of her heavily mascaraed eyelashes. "Is it very hard to get something like that started?"

Carly groaned at the hopeful tone. Most people thought opening a tiny shop like hers must be a snap. "Actually, it is. A small shop makes its money on far fewer items than a large store. If I make a mistake in choosing merchandise and something doesn't sell, it's a big loss for me."

"Oh." She was the picture of pouty disappointment.

"Alys, where is the file—?" Ty stopped in

the doorway. "What are you doing here?" he demanded.

"Looking for you." Carly crossed the vinyl flooring and entered his office when he moved aside.

Ty watched her for a second, then turned back to the outer office. "Alys, would you go help Buck with the bill of lading on that shipment of beeves going out this afternoon?"

The girl frowned, clearly not liking the request, but she nodded. In a minute, they heard her leave.

"Sit down," Ty invited. From the window, he observed his office help as she walked across the stable yard.

"You don't trust your secretary overmuch," Carly observed.

He snorted wryly. "If I'd closed my door, she probably would have listened at the keyhole. She likes to know everything that goes on."

"Why do you keep her?"

"Martha is her grandmother. She asked me to give the girl a job. I agreed. Actually, Alys is a good worker, she's just curious about things. So's her grandmother. The grand-daughter gets it honestly.''

''Ah, yes, I remember. Elena said the women on the ranch knew everything about everybody.''

''They do.'' His eyes narrowed. ''So, what brings you out here?''

''Elena and Rodrigo.''

The dark brows rose in question.

''I need handcrafted items for my shop. Elena showed me a necklace one of her girls made for her. She said making jewelry was a family hobby. They even make their own beads.''

''That's right. They have a large family. That's how they give Christmas gifts to everyone.''

''I need a telephone number or directions to her house. She's on a rural route, and there are about fifty people in the county with the same last name.''

His gaze swept down her pink cotton skirt and white eyelet blouse trimmed in pink. She wore a pink clip to keep her hair out of her eyes. Her skin grew warm as if his gaze were a caress. She wished it was.

He removed an address book from a drawer. Looking inside, he wrote a number and address on a notepad, then tore off the top sheet and handed it to her.

"Thanks." She dropped it inside her purse. "Now about Rodrigo. Is he available?"

Ty leaned back in the chair and rolled the pen back and forth between his palms. "That's according to what you want him for," he said bluntly, as if suspicious of her motives.

She considered picking up a yardstick propped in a corner and whacking him across the head. "Why, to seduce him, of course."

He pushed upright and ambled around the desk, an odd smile playing at the corners of his mouth. "If you want a man, try me," he invited.

She shook her head. "You're too hard to handle."

His laughter mocked both of them. "Yes. If you laid hands on me, we would end up at the house."

In my bed was the rest of that sentence.

She met his eyes, and the air sizzled like a dozen eggs frying all at once. The tension escalated when neither would look away. The ringing of the telephone shattered the duel.

"Macklin," Ty snapped into the receiver. "Oh, hello, Tina. No, nothing's wrong. I was…thinking of something."

He flicked a glance at Carly, then turned his back partially to her while he discussed weekend plans. She grimaced at his broad shoulders. Trying not to listen, she wondered what it would be like to be part of a large, caring family. It was something she'd never had. She had her shop. That was the important thing.

"Uh, she's here now, as a matter of fact," Ty said.

Carly looked up. His sister-in-law had asked about her?

"Okay," Ty said, "I'll handle it. Yeah, I promise." He talked another moment and said goodbye. "Tina wants to know if you'll join us for the reception at the resort tomorrow night. There'll be a dinner, hosted by the owners. The Barretts. You've met them. You're invited to that, too. Tina says she will not take no for an answer." He waited.

"I hadn't planned on going." Carly noted he'd included himself as a member of the party. There was no way she was going to spend an evening with him.

"You'll hurt her feelings if you refuse. Besides," he added on a persuasive note, "the reception profits will go to the new theater. Think of it as a good deed."

"I don't think so."

"I already promised her I'd bring you," he announced as if that decided the issue.

She glared at him.

"The reception is at six. I'll pick you up at five. That should give us plenty of time to get there."

He was waiting for her to say no, she realized. She hated to be predictable. "All right," she agreed, and was pleased to see the flicker of surprise in his eyes. "My new address is—"

"I know where you live." He gave her a cool glance, daring her to make something of it. "Do you have a telephone?"

She gave him the number. It felt strange, sort of as though they were making a real date. But they weren't. His sister-in-law had forced him into it.

"Now," he said, taking up another line of thought, "what did you want with Rodrigo?"

"I want to see if he'd supply me with those tiny carvings he does from walnuts. They're exquisite. I'd like some larger pieces if he's willing, too."

"You're trying to steal my help," Ty complained.

"It's possible they could make a living doing this. But not right away. Would it be okay if I go out and look for him?"

"Yes. I know where he's working. I'll take you."

"I don't mind walking."

"It's a long way. Rodrigo is taking soil samples in one of the back pastures down by the river. We'll ride."

She gave in gracefully. Not that it would have done any good to do otherwise. Ty Macklin was a law unto himself.

Outside, he motioned toward his truck. They climbed aboard. He drove around to the stable. "Wait here." He hopped out.

William, now in charge of the horses, came to the open door. He and Ty talked a few minutes, then went inside.

Ty returned with two paper cups of lemonade. After handing one to her, he took off again. Glancing back, she saw William standing in the shadows inside the stable, watching them. It gave her a funny feeling.

''Thanks,'' she murmured, and took a refreshing sip. It reminded her of the first kiss between them. He'd had lemonade with his dinner. The taste had lingered in his mouth, sweet and tart. She stole a glance at his lips.

He was preoccupied with his own thoughts as he drove over the dirt track that wound down to the river.

Her eyes were drawn again to his lips when he took another drink. The air was suddenly cooler. She realized they'd entered the woods and were traveling down the long row of shade produced by the oaks. Rolling down the window, she could hear the intimate murmuring of the water.

Ty turned left along the stream and followed the path there. It was very pleasant. She took another sip and again looked at her companion…at his mouth.

She liked the way his lips were shaped, clear cut and sensuous in a masculine way. They'd been firm but gentle on hers that second time, when she'd been injured. She wondered what a third embrace would be like...gentle...or maybe rougher...harder...

He flicked her a glance. "Keep it up, and you'll find out."

The air felt charged with electricity all of a sudden. "Find out what?" She nervously poked a long strand of hair under the clip that held the heavy mass away from her face.

"What you're wondering about."

"How...?" Her voice was husky. She had to clear it. "How do you know what I'm wondering about?"

He gave her another of his quick, dark glances. "Because I'm wondering the same."

"Which is?" She tried to sound amused.

"What another kiss between us would be like," he stated flatly, almost as if he resented the fact.

She refused to be daunted. "Lucky guess," she murmured, and gave him a deliberately wicked sideways glance.

The pickup stopped dead. She slid forward on the seat. An arm caught her around the middle, and she was aware of body heat and jeans pressed against her leg, of the feel of cotton under her hands as she held on to him.

"What is it?" she said, a whisper on the river wind. The question held all her doubts about her actions with him.

His eyes held a lethal gleam. For a second, her composure slipped. Teasing a tiger wasn't always a safe proposition.

"Go ahead," he invited. "Find out."

She blinked. He expected her to kiss him? She contemplated his lips. It was one thing to think about kissing someone, she discovered, but something else to do it...sort of like letting the tiger out of his cage. She thought she could control it...him, but she wasn't positive....

Drawing a calming breath, she flung her head up and gave him a daredevil smile. "What makes you think I'd want to?"

"You've been staring at my mouth since you got here. Afraid to chance it now that you have the opportunity?" His breath flowed warmly over her lips as he mocked her hesitation.

"Afraid? Of a kiss? Not on your life." She pressed her mouth to his. "See? Nothing to it."

"Now let's try it my way," he muttered savagely.

He took her lips in an openmouthed, moist, demanding kiss, a lover-to-lover kiss, a restraint-be-damned kiss. She was seized by the insane hope that it would never end.

Raising her arms, she looped them around his neck, dug her fingers into his thick, tawny hair and kissed him back for all she was worth. He gave a throaty groan and pulled her closer, one hand moving restlessly over her back while the other tangled in the long fall of hair down her spine.

The feel of his strong, lithe body did things to her sense of balance. If she hadn't been sitting, she'd have fallen. If she hadn't been clinging to him, she'd have tumbled from the seat.

When he at last drew back, they were both breathing hard. She opened her eyes slowly, afraid to look at him.

Suddenly, his attention shifted to a point behind her. "Oh, hell," he said, "there's Martha, glaring from her front porch."

The rapturous moment was ended. She hid

her disappointment. "Will she scold you for taking advantage of me?"

"You're quick on the uptake."

"I learned early to listen to what people meant, not what they said," she quipped.

"As an orphan living in foster homes?"

Was that a husky tenderness in his voice, or was she imagining it? "I didn't live in foster homes. I stayed with relatives until Aunt Essie took me in and kept me."

He twisted around, one arm resting on the seat behind her, the other draped over the steering wheel. His face was close to hers. She had only to lean a bit forward and their lips would touch....

A finger pressed her chin. "If I kiss you again, I'll drag you over to that grassy spot by the river and make love to you."

With an audience, she knew she was safe. "No, you won't. Martha would call the local sheriff and have you arrested for licentious behavior. Your family would be embarrassed."

"There's a willow whose branches come all the way to the ground. It's like another world. I used to hide in there and pretend I was on another planet when I was a kid."

She turned from him, using the time to compose herself. The willow tree was really there. "I can't imagine you as a child."

"We all start out the same in life." He started the truck again and drove on down the winding path by the river until they came to the pasture. He drove up to the electric fence and tapped the horn twice.

Rodrigo stopped working and looked up.

"Can you come here for a moment?" Ty called.

When the younger man arrived, Ty let Carly do the talking. She explained her idea in full.

"You want me to make things? To sell? People would pay money to buy my things?" The idea had obviously never occurred to him.

"Yes, they will," Carly assured him. "People on vacations love to buy things that are actually made in the area. You'll have to decide what your signature will be. You would be an inspiration to other artists, too. I'd like to develop a steady source of local crafts and goods."

Rodrigo looked at Ty. Ty hesitated, then nodded. "It sounds like a good deal. Carly will give you a fair price. It's up to you if you want to try it.''

"You can work on your carvings in your spare time,'' Carly said. She grinned. "Until you get to be rich and famous, then you'll have to build a studio and do it full-time.''

"Me?'' Rodrigo questioned.

"Yes, you. I think visitors will love your tiny animals. They'll buy them as gifts to take home to their family. Your price will go up and up, and I'll no longer be able to afford you.''

"But where would I sell then?'' he asked, already worrying about the future of his business.

She and Ty laughed together. She glanced at him, then away. She could fall in love with his laughter, deep and sort of gritty sounding. He was way too appealing for her comfort.

They planned a delivery date around Rodrigo's work schedule. Carly told him how much she would pay for each carving to start off. "Then we'll just have to wait and see how it goes.''

"And Elena is going to do jewelry?'' he asked.

"I hope so. I'm going to ask if she and her girls would like to try it."

Ty listened as Carly made her deal. The breeze brought the scent of her light perfume to him. He took a deep breath as a shaft of desire hit him anew.

He tightened a fist as resentment surged through him. Damn her and her soft lips and smart mouth. If he had any sense, he'd stay as far away from this river witch as possible.

River witch. There were stories he'd read as a kid about the mysterious enchantresses. Each river had its own witch. They were the spirit of the water, and they coveted other spirits, luring them into their cool, liquid depths with their siren embraces.

A man had to be careful around women like that or he'd get sucked in over his head before he knew what was what. Sometimes, he even wanted to. He forced his mind back to the present.

"I'll see you next week, then," Carly was saying. She and Rodrigo shook hands formally. The deal was done.

He started the engine, suddenly needing to

get Carly back to the office so she could leave before he did something stupid.

Her expression changed subtly, and he knew she understood he wanted to get rid of her. He nodded to Rodrigo, let the two say their farewells and started the engine. In a minute, they were on the gravel road that ran between two fields, a shorter way back to the main house. Dust kicked up behind them in a long white plume.

''I liked the river path better,'' his companion said.

''This gets us back faster.''

''So you can get rid of me.''

He clamped his teeth together and nodded. Anger roiled around in him like a loose cannon looking for a place to explode. The problem was he wanted to kiss her again. And she knew it.

''That's right,'' he told her. ''You're dangerous to my health.''

She gave him a cold stare. ''Last time I had a checkup, I didn't have anything contagious.''

''My mental health,'' he supplied.

He heard her give a snort of disdain, but she didn't say any more on the subject of him and her. He had to hand it to her—she played fair. She didn't badger a man into admitting his passion for her or use it against him. At least, she hadn't yet.

Give her time, he advised himself, adopting a cynical attitude about the whole stupid situation. He groaned under his breath. He had a week to get through, then that damned reception and dinner before she'd be out of his hair. Maybe he could make it through the weekend without exploding. But he doubted it....

Carly dressed in yellow cotton slacks with a yellow-striped blouse on Friday. She was going to the Rocking M to pick up her first pieces from Rodrigo and was quite excited about it.

Ha! she mocked herself. Lie to others but not to yourself. She was excited at the thought she might see Ty.

After tying her hair back with a big, floppy bow, she surveyed herself critically. With a clip-on sun visor shading her eyes and a clip-on purse around her waist, she was ready for a busy day of collecting items she'd ordered from various craftsmen around the county.

At a quarter to one, she arrived at the ranch

and parked in her usual spot. She found Rodrigo in the ranch office, flirting outrageously with Alys, who was also dressed in pants today—skintight and lethal.

"Good afternoon," she said, quickly closing the door to the air-conditioned office. "Thanks for meeting me."

Rodrigo laid a hand over his heart. "The boss so ordered. I but obey."

His dramatic spiel caused Alys to giggle appreciatively. Carly smiled, too. Rodrigo was a natural ham.

"Do you have the carvings ready?"

"He does," Alys answered for him. "They're beautiful."

They were. A family of tiny deer was so endearing, Carly wasn't sure she could bear to part with them. "These will have to go together as a grouping," she declared.

Ty appeared when she finished her business. He walked her to the car.

She glanced at her watch. She had time to stop by two more places, then she had to get home, take a shower and change for the reception.

"Don't forget our date tonight." He

smoothly reached around her and opened the car door, his arm brushing hers as he did. She jerked away and slid inside.

"You've made some people around here very happy and excited about their future," he observed. It didn't exactly sound like a compliment.

"Well, I'm happy, too. I think the store will do well for all of us." She was tired but pleased from a week of hard work.

He stepped aside and closed the door. She rolled the window down. "I'll see you at five."

She cranked up. "I could drive to the resort and meet you there. It would save you the trip to Yreka."

"My mother taught me a gentleman always calls at the door for his date." He gave her a sardonic smile.

"Date?" she questioned. "I think of it more as a favor to your sister-in-law."

His expression hardened. "Right."

She glanced in the rearview mirror when she drove off. He was standing with his hands thrust into his back pockets, his eyes on her as she left.

Later that day, on the way home, she thought about the situation between them. It was volatile. She didn't kid herself about that. He was a hard, cynical man. A sane woman wouldn't waste her time trying to change him.

She arrived at her apartment and let herself in. Glancing at the clock, she muttered, "Ohmygosh," and headed for the shower, strewing clothing over the bedroom floor as she did.

Thirty minutes later, she stood in front of her closet, peering into its depths like a miner searching for gold. She finally decided on a shimmery, champagne-colored dress with a sequined jacket of crimson. It glittered with every movement.

She slipped on the dress and black patent evening sandals, then put on makeup. After trying an elaborate hairdo, she gave up and put it up in a twist on top of her head, leaving a few long strands to waft carelessly down her neck and at her temples. With her watch and gold dangly earrings, she was ready.

The doorbell rang. Her heart took a nosedive to her toes. Resolving not to let Ty undermine her control, she picked up the jacket and a black beaded purse before going to the door.

He was wearing a dark evening suit. The slight natural curl in his tawny hair had been tamed to smooth waves flowing back from his forehead. He was incredibly handsome.

"Ah, your James Bond outfit," she quipped to cover her nervous state. At his questioning glance, she pointed to his tie. "James always wore a black silk knitted tie when he dressed up, too."

"You seem to know him well."

"I was in love with him from the time I was twelve until I was about sixteen. That's when I realized his girlfriends always came to some horrible end."

"True," Ty agreed, looking her over. "You've grown."

"High heels." She twisted one foot to the side so he could see the strappy evening shoes.

His gaze swept down and grazed along her leg to settle on her ankle. She suddenly felt self-conscious, as if she were showing off for him or something.

"Well, I'm ready," she said brightly, and

waited for him to step aside so she could leave and lock the door.

He continued to gaze at her for another moment, then as if giving himself a mental shake, he moved back and let her out.

"I need to stop by the house and see Jonathan for a minute. Do you mind?"

"Of course not." She gave in to curiosity. "Who's keeping him tonight?"

"Martha."

"Ah, yes, the voice of your conscience." With the teasing remark, she felt more at ease.

He seemed to sense it. He gave her a once-over, grinned and concentrated on driving the late-model luxury car.

They drove up the highway to the county road and took the exit there. His son was playing in the front yard when they arrived and ran to meet the car when it stopped.

"Did you get it?" he asked.

Ty smiled and reached down to pop open the trunk. "See for yourself." He slid out of the car and went to the back.

"Thanks, Dad."

Carly looked out the back window when the trunk closed. She saw Jonathan had a rope, which he was uncoiling and trying to get started in a twirl. He'd talked his dad into letting him take the roping lessons. She smiled, glad for the boy.

''Did you brush your pony down before you put him away?'' Ty asked his son.

''He's a *horse*,'' Jonathan corrected with proper indignation. ''I brushed him really clean and checked his hooves, too.''

''Good. I've got to go. Get to bed on time and brush your teeth. I'd better not get a bad report on you in the morning.''

Ty bent down and embraced his son. They kissed each other on the cheeks and hugged before saying good-night.

The scene brought tears to Carly's eyes. He could be so tender with his son. With sudden insight, she knew he'd been the same with his wife when they'd first married...when love was new and wonderful. She looked away, feeling like an intruder.

When they were on their way and he was busy with the heavy traffic on the interstate highway, she studied him surreptitiously.

''What are you thinking now?'' he suddenly demanded, causing her to jump guiltily.

"Nothing."

"Don't give me that. You're trying to figure something out."

"Well, I was wondering how you could be so gentle and yet so hard at the same time."

"Gentle? I've never been that."

"With your son, you are."

His mouth softened momentarily. "Kids are different. They don't lie. And they don't use your love against you. Treat them decently, and they'll love you forever."

"You were close to your family," she concluded. "Even though your father made you work."

"Yes."

She heard a wealth of meaning in the word. She realized he missed them. For the briefest moment, she envisioned putting down roots on this land...with this man.

"My earliest memories are of sitting by a fire on a cold night," he went on in a nostalgic vein. "We'd have a big bowl of popcorn that my mother had made. Shane and I would be stretched out on the rug. My parents would take turns reading to us."

"What kind of stories did you like?" she asked quietly.

"All kinds—adventure, fantasy, sports. I even liked *Little Women* when my mom read it to us one winter. I cried when the youngest one died."

"Yes, so did I." Carly envisioned him as a boy. He'd have been rather like Jonathan, she thought. Daring and self-confident. Friendly and outgoing, his blue eyes taking in his world eagerly.

He'd probably never been lonely and scared, not the way she'd been when she'd gone to live with her aunt and uncle, the ones who'd finally agreed to take her in "for a while."

No one had wanted the silent, unsmiling child on a permanent basis. Until Aunt Essie.

"It must be nice to have a big family," she mused aloud.

"Poor little orphan," he mocked, yet his tone wasn't unkind. "It can also be hell, especially if you're the youngest. Someone is always telling you what to do."

"Did Shane boss you around?"

"He tried to."

"I'll bet you fought with him."

"He gave me more than one bloody nose. My dad would send us both to the stables and make us muck out all the stalls."

"Your father was a very wise man."

Ty seemed to consider. After a moment, he nodded. "I think he was. He was tough but fair. He was always gentle with my mother, though. He adored her. When she died—"

He stopped abruptly.

Carly knew he'd disclosed more than he'd meant to about his family. Ty had been a teenager when his mom had died.

"I'm sorry," she said simply. "I know how it hurts."

He pulled into a parking space at the resort. "How did we get on such a morbid subject?" He swung out of the car and came around to help her out. "It's cool up here. You'll need your jacket."

He took it from her and held it while she slipped it on. His fingers brushed her neck lightly as he settled it on her shoulders.

Heat rushed to the spot, then spiraled down into the innermost parts of her. She hated to go inside. It had been nice, talking quietly to him about the past, sharing the loneliness.

She took a shaky breath. Loneliness wasn't a basis for a relationship. So what was? She was afraid to answer that.

Chapter Eight

The reception was in full swing when Carly and Ty arrived. Genny Barrett rushed forward to greet them. "I'm so glad you could come. Tina said to expect you. She and Shane are sitting on the sofa where the crowd is. You'll have to fight your way through to them. Rafe and I will talk to you later."

"Right," Ty said to their hostess as she turned to greet the next arrivals, then took Carly's arm and guided her across the crowded room. Each person had paid fifty dollars for the ticket to the reception and the play that would be staged next week.

"This turnout should earn quite a bit for the

new theater and ensure a large audience for the new production,'' he remarked to Carly as they wound their way through the huge room. ''Do you want a drink?''

''Yes, please.''

He changed their course and headed for the bar. ''What would you like?''

She recalled that he had once been a heavy drinker. The thought made her uneasy. ''A ginger ale.''

He ordered her drink and a club soda. He cast her an oblique glance. ''Except for a beer or wine, which we'll probably have with our meal, I gave up hard liquor three years ago.''

''When you were divorced and you had your son to take care of on your own?'' She was guessing.

Annoyance flared over his handsome face and was gone. ''Don't you ever keep your thoughts to yourself?''

''Sorry. The timing fit.''

''You're right. Jonathan needed a father he could depend on. I'd do anything for my son.''

''Including marrying again?'' she asked curiously. She studied his face as he paid the bar bill.

He handed her a glass. "No," he said, so deadly quiet she knew he meant it.

The room seemed darker all at once. She managed a gay lilt of laughter. "I was told to watch out for you, that you change your women the way most men change their shirts." She took a sip of ginger ale. It was icy cold and felt good to her tight throat.

He shrugged. "I've found that women build up expectations when a man sees them more than once or twice."

"You've made it plain to me that anything more than the moment is out. Didn't you warn them, too?"

He slugged down a drink of club soda. "Yeah, but some don't listen. They can't believe a man doesn't need a woman to manage his life and fortune."

"Jonathan thinks you do."

"Jonathan is a child."

Carly deliberately looked him over. "And you're not."

"No. And you damned well know it." He gave her a grin that was both arrogant and endearing. "Let's go see if we can have a snack. For fifty bucks apiece, we should get really great food, maybe some of those little hot dogs wrapped in a biscuit," he added facetiously, causing her to laugh.

She laughed again when they reached the refreshment table. The cocktail wieners, wrapped in a pastry crust, were neatly stacked in rows on a tray.

"Here. You hold the drinks. I'll get the food."

She took his glass in her right hand.

"You have a very alluring laugh," he told her, piling food on a tiny plate, his gaze flicking briefly to her mouth.

She stopped smiling. This was dangerous, being with him, enjoying the moment with no thought of tomorrow. It would take so little to send them both over the edge....

"Not too much," she reminded him when the stack of food threatened to overflow the plate. "We have dinner yet to go." She took a drink of his club soda by mistake, made a face and sipped the ginger ale.

"Believe me, it will be at least nine before we eat."

He was right. It was ten minutes before the hour before they and the other two couples left the reception, which showed no signs of ending soon, and retired to a private dining room.

"Oh, that was fun," Tina said, sinking into a comfortable chair, her maternity top flaring around her as she did. She kicked off her shoes and stretched her toes.

She was dressed in a deep red outfit. Her eyes and skin glowed. Picture of a woman in love, Carly thought. Shane didn't hover too much, but he kept an eye on his wife and was always close in case she needed an arm to lean on.

Ty, Carly noted, was also attentive to his sister-in-law. He brought her a glass of water while Carly drifted to the window and looked outside at the moonlit landscape.

She wondered if he harbored any lingering feelings for his brother's wife. He'd thought he was in love with her at one time, according to the ranch women.

That had been ages and ages ago, when he'd been but a lad of twenty-one. Fourteen years. She'd have been sixteen then. That had been the year her foster brother, Brody, came to live with Aunt Essie. She suddenly missed him. He was a year older than she was, the one who'd always listened to her chatter without complaining.

"Penny for them," Rafe Barrett said, coming to stand beside her at the window.

"I was thinking of my foster brother," she told him. She gestured to the magnificent scene outside the window. "He would love it here."

Night had settled in. Far away, lights twinkled in the valley, making it look magical. A fog bank was creeping up the river toward the small town tucked into a fold in the mountains.

"You're lonely for your family," he concluded, surprising her with his insight.

"Does it show?"

He shook his head. "Merely a guess on my part. My sister and I were raised in boarding schools. That was lonely, too."

"Where is your sister now?"

"She's married to one of the McPherson brothers. They have—"

"A ranch up near Crater Lake," she finished for him. "I read a story in the paper recently. One of the brothers taught a roping class the other day after school. Ty's son took part. Did you see it on the evening news?"

"Yes. Kids and calves running everywhere.

It was pretty funny. Kerrigan handled it well. He and Rachel and their two kids spent the weekend with us. I had a plaque made up for him.''

She laughed as he described the award, which he'd had engraved with Hero in large letters.

''Dinner,'' his wife announced after consulting with the waiter. They took their places at the table.

Ty's arm brushed hers as they were seated. His eyes met hers. She saw anger in them and wondered what was wrong. Perhaps Shane had mentioned something that upset him.

However, he seemed to get over it in a short time. She found she was enjoying the company immensely as the evening progressed and his smiles came more often. He even teased her about her ranching experiences when Shane brought the subject up.

''I was a very good worker. Admit it,'' she demanded.

''She was terrible,'' he told the others behind his hand and dodged the slap she playfully tried to deliver. ''She can't cook.''

When the waiter offered a brandy to Ty, he

refused. She hesitated. She wasn't light-headed, but she was feeling pretty happy. Perhaps she shouldn't overindulge.

"Go ahead," he murmured close to her ear. "I'm driving."

"Well, one more." She glanced at her watch. "It's midnight," she gasped in surprise.

"Going to turn into a cinder maid?"

"More likely a pumpkin," she corrected, patting back a yawn.

"Me, too," Tina said, also yawning. "Of course, I *am* a pumpkin." She made a comical face while the others laughed.

They chatted a bit longer over brandy and coffee, then walked down the steps and outside. Fog hung over the valley, gossamer and ethereal in the moonlight. Snow glittered on the peaks.

Shane and Tina said good-night and went to their car. Their host and hostess added their farewells and went toward the condos rising on the side of the hill like phantoms of the night.

"It's beautiful, isn't it?" Carly said on a catchy breath.

"Yes." But he wasn't looking at the scenery.

They walked to the car and started down the winding road into the valley. The fog closed around them, blurring the moonlight to a hazy glow. The taillights of Shane's vehicle winked in and out, then disappeared in front of them. On the interstate highway, the fog was worse. She felt safe and snug inside the warm car.

"I should have brought my car," she murmured, "then you wouldn't have to drive down to Yreka in this."

"Do you think I would let you drive it alone?"

She thought it over. "No," she said. "You're very gallant when it comes to women."

He gave a low snort. "Women don't like that sort of thing nowadays. It's old-fashioned to let a man take care of you. I don't suppose you plan on staying home and having babies once you're married." He gave her a quick look, then peered back at the road, which seemed to shift, too, as the fog moved across it.

"I don't think I'll ever marry. I'm going to

be a famous entrepreneur and—'' she smoth-
ered a huge yawn ''—and...I forgot what I
was saying.'' She lapsed into silence.

He slowed to a crawl. ''The fog is getting
worse,'' he muttered under his breath. It was
growing steadily worse as they neared the
river. Visibility was sometimes no more than
ten feet.

''Maybe we shouldn't try to get to my place.
Isn't there a motel at the next exit?'' She
squinted against the obscuring mist and tried
to remember where she'd seen the sign for the
place.

At the exit, they found the road was blocked
by the highway patrol. ''Bad accident down
the road,'' the trooper told them, recognizing
Ty. ''The highway is closed.''

''You have any idea how long it'll be before
it's cleared?''

The trooper shook his head. ''Not anytime
soon. It's a five-car pileup. This fog is a
killer.''

Carly felt sorry for the patrolman. He looked
tired. Ty took the exit. He stopped at the in-
tersection with the country road. ''There's a

back road to the ranch. You could stay at my place. That would be the sensible thing to do.''

Her heart stopped, then gave a giant lurch. She forced a nonchalant amusement into her reply. ''Don't sound so enthusiastic. I might think you want me.''

''I do. That's the problem,'' he said, sounding as snarly as a sore-tailed dog.

''I know. I want you, too.'' She sighed. Life could get in such an impossible coil.

He studied her in the dim light from the dash, then turned onto the road. A mile down it, he turned onto another road, one that was gravel. They crept up and down the fog-bound hills. The fifteen-mile trip took almost an hour. She realized he really was taking her to his house.

Well, it was the only practical thing to do, she decided while her insides curled into knots.

When they crossed the bridge and entered the long driveway that led to his house, her heart started thumping loudly. Ahead of them, the headlights barely cut through the fog.

It was a relief when the garage door slid open to let them inside. She felt both safe and vulnerable—safe because they'd escaped the fog without accident, vulnerable because she'd have to stay the night in his home, knowing he was close by.

The house was totally dark when they entered. Ty flicked a switch, and soft light brightened the hallway and the stairs. He led the way up the marble steps. "You can use this bedroom."

He touched the switch that turned on a lamp and stepped back for her to enter.

Carly glanced back down the steps. The house seemed curiously vacant. "Where's your baby-sitter?"

"Jonathan is spending the night with Martha and Buck."

"Oh," she said, then *"Oh"* as the implications hit her.

"Are you going to faint at the thought of being alone in the house with me?"

He waited, a mocking gleam in his eyes as she struggled with an answer. She wanted to demand to be taken home at once, but she wouldn't give him the satisfaction.

"Hardly," she replied with remarkable calm considering that her heart and lungs were working in fits and starts. "This room is fine. Could I borrow a T-shirt to sleep in?"

She held his gaze until he nodded. When he turned and walked down to the end of the hall, she entered the bedroom.

After laying her purse on a table, she removed the sequined jacket and laid it over the back of a chair. Then she stood in the center of the room with her hands cupped around her elbows while she waited for Ty to return.

Her gaze was drawn irresistibly to the bed.

The queen-size mattress was covered by a floral spread that matched the yellow, white and green print on the chair. The drapes were striped in the same hues. The sheer undercurtains were a soft golden beige.

A selection of books and solitaire-type puzzles and games was available in an oak bookcase flanking one of the windows. A small bureau and a lamp table next to the chair completed the furniture.

From the window, the fog eddied around the house like ghosts wearing ragged sheets. The low moan of the wind around the eaves caused her scalp to prickle and tighten.

She heard a sound behind her and whirled around with a gasp.

Ty stood in the doorway, watching her with a curious gaze. He held out a pajama top. "Will this do?"

She stared at the garment as if it might attack at any moment. "Uh, yes. Of course. Thank you." She took a step toward him.

His dark eyebrows went up fractionally as he dropped the nightshirt on the chair. He'd taken off his jacket and tie and rolled his shirt cuffs up. "Are you scared of the dark or something?"

Involuntarily, her gaze skittered to the window. She swallowed and shook her head.

"I think you are."

"No." She clasped her arms tightly against her, drawing inward as she reacted to emotions she couldn't name.

He crossed the polished wood floor and stood in front of her on the braided-rag rug. "You're trembling."

His voice was low and soothing, with the cadence of a lullaby. It strummed over her taut nerves like the bow of a violin held by a master musician. With quiet despair, she stepped forward.

"Would you hold me?" she whispered.

Several thoughts raced across his face, too fast to read. Something raw and elemental blazed into his eyes. "What if I can't let you go?" he asked quietly.

"Maybe I don't want you to." She managed a shaky smile.

He opened his arms. She took the step to bring her close. His arms closed around her, holding her but not pressing.

She clenched her hands on his shirt, gathering up the soft white cotton in her fists, then sighed as she leaned her head against his chest and closed her eyes.

In the silence, she could hear his heartbeat, solid and strong beneath her ear. After a minute, he rested his cheek on her head. The trembling quietened as his warmth seeped through her.

"You always smell so good," he murmured. "Like lemon basil, sort of sweet and tart at the same time, but with an undertone of spice. Your own special scent. I like it."

"Thank you."

"Do you remember that day you were shell-ing peas on the porch? You dropped one. I picked it up and ate it."

"Yes." She was so sleepy she could hardly talk. "You left right after that."

"I had to." His voice went deeper. "I wanted to...do things to you."

She lifted her head and stared at him. He smiled, and it tore at her heart. It was both wistful and cynical.

"You scare me," he confessed.

"Why?"

"Holding you reminded me of things I'd forgotten. I didn't want to remember how it felt to admire a woman, to want to share things with her."

"What things?"

"Quiet conversation, observations on life...things."

"I see." She laid her head against his chest again.

His hands moved over her back as he mas-saged the muscles at either side of her spine. Her head felt so heavy, as if the long fall of hair weighed a ton. Slowly, she let her head tilt back until she stared up at him again, her strength barely sufficient to hold her eyelashes up enough to see him.

"When you look at me like that," he whispered, almost to himself, "as if the world were filled with wonder, it makes me wonder what you would do if I kissed you."

"I think I would kiss you back."

He smiled slightly. "Would you?"

As the world stood still, he bent to her, not to her lips, but to her neck. He kissed her on the pulse that beat in her throat. A sigh escaped her, a tiny sound of need she couldn't suppress.

His hands tightened, then moved again. He stroked up and down her side with one hand, coming perilously close to her breast as he did. His lips continued to maraud her neck.

Tantalizing sensations shot over her from every caress. Acting purely on instinct, she moved, turning her body slightly so that his hand grazed the side of her breast.

But that wasn't enough, either. Impatient for more, she followed his hand when he would have moved it away.

Tension turned his body rigid for a second, then he slid his hand over, covering her breast with his palm. She sighed and arched against him.

"Want you," she heard herself say. Her body insisted on taking over from her common sense. She couldn't seem to find any willpower to assert at all. There was just this yearning....

"Do you?" He sounded shaken by her confession.

He kneaded her breast, and her nipple sprang up, greedy in its desire for more. She made a purring sound of pleasure.

"You're like a cat," he told her, "wanting to be petted."

She smiled. Turning her head, she kissed him through his shirt, then breathed against the material and felt the heat thus generated become trapped in the threads. She sucked in, drawing the heat away.

Under her searching fingers, she felt his nipple bead the way hers had. She gently ran her nails over it, then squeezed lightly.

He gave a throaty chuckle and pressed her hips against him. She felt his arousal near the apex of her thighs. With his hands cupped under her hips, he guided her as she brushed against him. Again. And again.

She wrapped her arms around his shoulders and buried her fingers in his hair. She tugged until he brought his head up, then she pressed forward until her mouth met his.

He moved suddenly, lifting her from the floor so that she was dependent on his strength to keep them upright. Kicking off her evening sandals, she wrapped her legs around his waist, wringing a pleased gasp from him. She felt him take three long strides, then she was falling....

They landed on the bed with a bounce of the springs. He absorbed his weight on one arm while he held her tucked close to him with the other. A wild gladness gathered in her while he ravished her face with kisses.

"Ty," she said.

He tensed abruptly. He raised his head and gazed at her. "Are you going to tell me to stop?"

She stared at him, at the dark passion in his eyes, the fire and the fury that blazed there, near the edge but not out of control. If she asked, she knew he would leave.

Giving a quick shake of her head, she slipped her hands between them and worked on his buttons. When she glanced back at him, there seemed to be tenderness, even gratitude, in his gaze. It make her feel oddly protective of him.

"I'm not going to stop," she murmured wickedly, "unless you tell me to."

"That might not be until morning," he warned.

"Good."

He let out a deep breath and brought one of her hands to his lips. He kissed the back of it, then the palm. "You're not going to play games."

"It's not my way," she said, halfway apologizing for not being like other women. She didn't know how to dissemble.

Pressing her hand to his chest, he moved to the side, one leg over both of hers. He rubbed his fingertips along the modest neckline of her dress. "I want to see you."

A tremor ran over her. She knew he could feel it, too, but she couldn't hide it. She wanted him more than she'd ever wanted anything in her life.

When she pulled his shirt from his slacks, he took her hands in one of his big ones and extended them over her head. "Zipper in the back?" he asked, kissing her throat as if fascinated with the taste and texture of her flesh there.

"Yes."

He let her hands go and searched at the back of her neck until he found the tab. He coaxed the zipper down, rolling sideways with her so that he could unfasten it all the way. She felt air hit her back as the dress opened. Another tremor rocked through her.

"Easy." He slipped his hand inside and rubbed the bare skin along her back. He found the strap across her back.

She felt her bra tighten, then loosen as he unhooked it. He laid her on the bed again and sat up, his weight on one arm. He eased the material off one shoulder, then the other, taking the undergarment with it. When she withdrew her arms, he let the silky material fall in folds at her waist.

The part of her that had learned to be careful, to not trust anyone too much, whispered a steady stream of caution. It was too late for that. She wanted him…and this night, no matter what might follow afterward.

For a long minute, he stared at her. "Beautiful," he said.

"I'm not very…I'm sort of…small."

"Beautiful," he repeated. "Perfect." He moved down until his face was level with her breasts, then he took one into his mouth.

She closed her eyes tightly as sensation, almost like pain, spiraled from the point of contact into all parts of her. She put her hands on his head, not sure whether she was going to pull him closer or push him away.

With a moan, she held him close and let him take his fill of her. He lavished his attention equally, thrilling her with his soft words of pleasure, his ardent words of praise.

His hands moved over her, stroking her arm, covering one breast while he suckled and teased the other. He slipped his leg between her thighs, moving against her just enough to drive her senseless with hints of the bliss to come.

She strained against him, demanding more.

"Relax," he urged with a soundless laugh. "It will be there for you."

"Will it?" In her desperation, she wasn't sure.

He paused and looked down at her, studying her mouth before going to her eyes. "Don't you believe me?"

Laying her hand over his, she stilled his motion on her taut breast. "I don't know."

His eyes narrowed. "Your past lovers haven't been very considerate if they didn't see that you got your pleasure first."

"There was only one—" She clamped her lips together. She didn't want to reveal her past, how stupid she'd been, thinking there must be love....

"On a scale of one to ten, how much satisfaction did you get?" Ty asked.

She felt the heat rush up her neck into her face. She managed a cheeky grin. "On a scale of one to ten? About zero."

He muttered an expletive.

"Well, it wasn't that bad."

He brushed across her lips with his, a tease of a kiss. "Hush, darling. This time will be different. I guarantee it."

The careful, cautious part of her curled up and blew away at his promise. For whatever reason, she trusted Ty Macklin. If he promised rapture, there would be rapture.

Letting go of his hand, she touched his jaw, letting her fingertips trace the strong line to his chin. She rubbed his bottom lip, liking the shape of it.

He nipped at her and caught her finger between his teeth. Watching her, he sucked on it, his tongue playing lazy games on the very tip.

Taking a deep breath, she ducked her head and buried her face in the dark brown curls on his chest. She found his nipple and did to it what he was doing to her fingertip. It beaded against her tongue, filling her with sudden delight. She laughed.

He released her finger. "Witch," he said, nuzzling through her hair. He caught a handful of it. "It looks like spilled ink, your hair. It's soft. Soft like you. All over. I didn't know anything could be so soft, so sweet."

Catching her close, he found her mouth. Soon that wasn't enough, either. Not for her. Not for him.

"Let's get really comfortable, shall we?" he invited. He slipped her dress over her hips, skimmed it along her legs and tossed it toward the chair when it came free.

His eyes sizzled over her, taking in her lacy

briefs, widening slightly at the beige garter belt, then crinkling as he smiled. "Let's see if I can work one of these...."

He reached behind her to unhook it, then he pulled it, the stockings and the briefs off in one jumble. They went the way of the dress, joining it on the floor where it had fallen.

"You," she said, wanting him naked, too.

When he'd kicked off his shoes, she rose to her knees and helped with his clothing, laughing as they got in each other's way. She stared in fascination when his powerfully built body was revealed for her perusal. The laughter faded away to quickening breaths. She'd never wanted anyone so much.

He threw the bedspread toward the foot of the bed, then eased her down on the smooth, pale green sheets. Propping himself on one arm, he spread her hair over the pillow, evenly covering it with the black tresses.

"Wait," he said, frowning suddenly. He slid off the bed while she looked at him in confusion. "I'll be back."

She bit her lip as he left the room, wondering why he'd walked out but somehow knowing he would return. He did. After laying several packets on the lamp table located between the bed and the chair, he rejoined her.

"Now," he said, and there was a wealth of meaning in the word.

She trembled when he gathered her close, but he didn't give her time to think on it. He went straight to her mouth and kissed her until they were both breathless, his mouth slanting first one way, then another across hers in reckless play.

His tongue invaded her mouth, and there were new games to be tried between them, she discovered as they dueled and tasted and licked at each other.

When his caresses glided down her torso to her thighs, she wondered if she could take much more. Each touch generated such a fierce rush of sensation, she felt she might faint if it became any more intense.

Instinctively, her body twisted to meet his, pressing against his hard length, feeling the gentle thrusting on her thigh. She wanted him inside her, filling her with the joy of that joining....

"Please," she whispered against his lips.

Ty shuddered at her heated response. She

was hot under his hands. Carefully, he explored her heat, finding her moist and receptive to his touch. When he rubbed the sensitive nub, she stiffened slightly, then burrowed against him. Her hand went to him, urging him into her depths.

"Not yet," he told her. "Not until you need it more than air, more than life itself...the way I need you." His voice was gruff, straining now with his own needs, holding himself in check with an effort. Her first, then both of them together.

"Yes," he heard himself saying past the roar of blood in his ears. She bucked against him, demanding fulfillment. "Don't rush. It'll be...incredible."

"Please," she said again, and raked her nails over his hips, not hurting but sending shafts of pleasure through him.

"All right, darling," he tried to soothe her. She whimpered when he moved away. He grabbed a packet and ripped it open.

Before he could remove the condom, she lifted it from the foil. With shaking hands, she put it into position. When she proved awkward, he experienced a strange sense of tenderness for her, for her eagerness, for her wish to take part in their lovemaking as an equal with him.

He guided her hands in the procedure. When he was ready, he leaned over her, sliding over to rest between her legs. He was acutely aware of her rapt gaze as he let his hips sink toward hers.

Holding himself up with his arms, he nudged the outer portals, sensing she wanted to see their joining. ''Take me in.''

She met his glance, then looked back at the place of contact. With a little purr of excitement, she fit their bodies together. He smiled at her eagerness when her hips rose off the bed, demanding that he come inside…to the warmth…to a welcome he'd never dreamed possible.…

''Ahhh,'' he groaned, and closed his eyes and thought of cold mountain streams and banks of snow to cool his blood.

When he was buried as deeply as he could go, they lay still. Regaining his breath, he reached between them and teased her with his thumb until she writhed beneath him. She roamed his chest and neck with her lips, laving trails of moist lava to burn right through his control.

He caught her wandering mouth with his, holding his body still while she rippled beneath him like waves from a wild storm. When her hands stopped roaming and clamped tightly to his arms, he increased the pressure of his thumb and moved in short bursts against her. She cried out against his mouth.

Shuddering, he waited out the tempest, refusing to give in to his own needs just yet. He wanted more for her, from her. He wanted…he didn't know what he wanted, but he knew he had to search, to explore every element of this strange, sweet passion that existed between them…between him and this woman.

Chapter Nine

Carly woke as Ty eased away from her. She opened her eyes and followed his tall form as he walked to the window. The sun was a brilliant disk well above the horizon, its rays lighting the underside of a billowy cloud to pale shades of gold.

When she scooted up against the pillows, he turned and saw her watching him. Their eyes locked. When he didn't smile or offer a greeting, she didn't, either. She didn't know what to say about the most shattering experience of her life.

"Did you sleep okay?" he finally asked as

if recalling that he was the host and she the guest. "I meant to go to my bed...."

His voice trailed off. She knew he was remembering when he'd started to leave during the night. She'd tightened her arms around him and refused to let go. He'd sighed, kissed her and stayed.

"Yes. You?" She couldn't tear her eyes away from his lean, muscular body. With the glow from the window outlining his naked splendor, he reminded her of a magnificent creature from long ago, wary, alert and wise in the ways of the ancient world.

He made a throaty sound, almost a growl, then he strode over, swept the sheet from her and lifted her into his arms. Startled, she threw her arms around his neck and held on. He carried her down the hall to his room.

There, he kicked the door shut behind them and headed for the shower. With warm water trailing over them, he shampooed her hair and rubbed a creme rinse into the long tresses, smoothing the tangles out with his fingers.

She'd never shared a bath with a man. It had its own sensual pleasures, she found, which Ty amply demonstrated to her. When their bath was finished and he'd dried them both off, he loaned her a toothbrush.

"Hardly been used," he said.

Smiling, she took it from him. They stood side by side at the twin sinks while they brushed. To her, the morning ritual seemed more intimate than the physical intimacy of the night in a way. Sharing the start of the day promised a future that hadn't been mentioned during the long night of passion.

When they finished, he caught her up in his arms again. She sighed with pleasure as he carried her to his bed.

"My bed...the guest-room bed," she corrected, "is already, uh, mussed up." She couldn't think of a delicate way to phrase it.

He smiled, his first of the morning. "And women hate to see a bed unmade for no good reason." He headed out the door. "Did anyone ever mention you talk in your sleep?" he inquired as he walked down the hall with her.

"No." She raised her head from his shoulder and peered anxiously into his eyes. "What did I say?"

"Oh, nothing incriminating. You must have

been dreaming about the shop. You murmured something about a work of art.''

He dumped her on the bed and followed her down, his body covering hers as he settled his mouth on hers before she could say a word.

And then, of course, words weren't necessary for what came next, although they each murmured several over the next hour.

Carly sat at the table in the kitchen while Ty cooked bacon and sausage. Batter steamed in the waffle iron, an old-fashioned round one that had belonged to his grandmother. Her image of him shifted again. He was perfectly at ease in the kitchen.

Except for an occasional fling, he had no need for a woman on a permanent basis, she realized. She turned her attention back to the paper he'd insisted she read while he prepared the meal.

She felt rather self-conscious idling at the table while he did all the work. Of course, with her cooking, that was the safest course.

When the telephone rang, she jumped, feeling odd about anyone finding out she was here. Ty answered on the second ring.

"I'm fixing waffles. Mm-hmm. Tell Martha it's okay with me if you come on home. Bye." He replaced the receiver. "Jonathan is going to join us for breakfast."

She jumped out of the chair as if it were a hot seat. "Uh, perhaps I should make up the bed. Shall I put on fresh sheets?"

His amused glance mocked her sudden case of nerves. She felt as if Aunt Essie were about to catch her in some mischief. He studied her face for a long second. "Clean sheets are in the hall closet," he told her.

She hurried up the steps into the hall. When she returned to the kitchen a few minutes later, she carried an armload of pale green cotton percale. "Where should I put these?"

"The washing machine is through that door."

His eyes were laughing. Her face warmed. She ignored him and went into the small room off the kitchen.

It contained a utility sink of stainless steel, a freezer and a gleaming white washer-and-dryer set. She stuffed the sheets in the machine, added soap and pushed the button to start.

"For a modern career woman, you're surprisingly inhibited," Ty remarked. He removed a crisp brown waffle from the iron and poured more batter. "Jonathan wouldn't notice if every bed in the house had been slept in."

The six-year-old probably wouldn't, but she felt better with things looking tidy. Just in case.

"He'll probably wonder why you're wearing my shirt, though," Ty warned her.

She looked down at her attire. Ty had loaned her a T-shirt and a pair of elastic-waisted cutoffs, which clung to her hips with no assurance of staying up. The slightest tug would dislodge them. She was barefoot.

With no makeup and her hair pulled into a ponytail, she must look a mess. Her hands went to her lips. She hadn't even put on lipstick after they'd left her bed the last time.

"You look fine," Ty said, bringing a plate to the table. "Wholesome. Like a farm girl."

"I am a farm girl." She suddenly wanted him to know about her life. "My aunt had a few acres. We had a cow for milk and butter, and chickens for fresh eggs."

"You can milk?" he asked, astounded.

"Yes. And plow and plant a vegetable garden. We canned quarts of food every year. It was fun. My foster brother and I would do the picking, cleaning and whatever else needed doing while Aunt Essie supervised and did most of the actual canning with a pressure canner. It used to scare me when the pot started hissing, and steam would make the gauge on top jiggle." She laughed. "I kept a wary eye on it."

He shook his head. "I can't imagine you being afraid of anything, not after that fracas with Hodkin."

"I'm not afraid of people."

"Maybe you should be." He stopped when a vehicle pulled into the driveway and parked. A minute later, Jonathan came running into the house. Shane entered behind him and closed the kitchen door.

"I picked up a hitchhiker on your driveway," the sheriff said with an easy smile, nodding toward the boy.

"Hi," Jonathan called to Carly. He climbed on a bar stool at the counter and peered at the waffle sections on a plate. "Boy, do those smell good, Dad. Can I have one now?"

"Sure. Take this plate to the table and join Carly. You two can eat before the waffle gets cold. Shane, you hungry?"

"Well, I had cereal earlier—"

"You better have one of these, Uncle Shane," Jonathan advised. "Dad makes the best."

"In that case, you talked me into it."

"What are you doing up so early?" Ty asked his brother.

"Fishing. I caught a mess of trout. I thought you might join us for an early supper." Shane's blue eyes cut to her. "You, too, Carly," he said easily.

"I may have some work to do tonight," she said, unable to think of any excuse not to, but not certain Ty wanted her.

Shane poured a cup of coffee, took the plate Ty handed him and seated himself at the table. He pushed the syrup pitcher toward Carly. She realized she hadn't started eating. She picked up her fork and joined Jonathan and Shane. In a minute, Ty came over with a platter of meat and extra waffle sections. He stacked two wedges on his plate, generously covered them with syrup and dug in.

After the first bite, she ate hungrily, too. The meal was delicious. Ty had a multitude of talents, it seemed.

"The fog was thick last night, wasn't it?" Shane remarked.

She paused in the act of taking a bite.

"Yes, it was," Ty answered.

She relaxed.

"There was a bad wreck on the interstate near Ashland. The traffic was tied up for a couple of hours." He looked from Ty to Carly. "It was a wise decision to stay here."

A blush started midway down her chest and climbed to her face, then rose all the way to her scalp.

"I made the decision to bring her here," Ty said in a casual tone. "She didn't have a choice."

"Sleep-overs are fun," Jonathan declared with an enthusiastic smile. "Did Dad make popcorn balls for you? He did the last time I had some guys over. He let us stay up practically all night and talk. Did you get to stay up late?"

His innocent questions made Carly squirm. "Well—"

"It was pretty late when we got in," Ty broke in. "Carly went to bed right away."

"Did she sleep in your room?"

She nearly dropped her fork. Looking at the boy, she could detect no guile in his expression. He was merely curious. Shane was seized by a coughing fit and hid his face behind his napkin.

"She stayed in the guest room," Ty said truthfully.

"Yes," Carly said, nodding several times. "I did."

A buzzer went off on the washing machine. Carly froze. She stared at the utility-room door as if expecting Martians to appear. Jonathan went on happily eating his breakfast.

"I washed the sheets," she said lamely. She rushed from the kitchen into the utility room. Behind the door, she pressed her hands to her hot cheeks and wondered how she'd gotten herself into such a ridiculous situation.

"Carly is very conscientious," she heard Ty say on a strangely wry note. "She likes to tidy everything up before she leaves."

She switched the sheets and pillowcases to the dryer, threw in a nonstatic tissue and set the timer for thirty minutes. There was nothing else to keep her from returning to the table.

With a calming breath, she went out. Ty's brother met her quick glance with a smile. He was enjoying the debacle; that much was obvious. What wasn't clear were his thoughts on the subject.

His smile was kind. More than that, his gaze seemed to be approving, as if he were encouraging her, but in what way? What did he want her to do? Help Ty over his distrust of women?

That might be more than any woman was capable of doing. Ty had deep-seated suspicions regarding the motives of the fairer sex, and not without reason, she had to admit.

She had some serious doubts about the man-woman relationship herself. Neither of them had had great experiences with the opposite sex. Would the sheriff help her over her distrust, too?

Against her own advice, she'd gotten involved in another person's life, a thing she'd vowed not to do. She gazed at Ty, wondering about his thoughts on this, the morning after the most shattering experience she'd ever had.

She had considered a month-long fling, but

this promised to be more. Suddenly, she couldn't imagine a future without him in it....

"This is fun, isn't it, Carly?" Jonathan commented.

She was perched on top of a horse that Ty said was very well behaved. She wasn't so sure. He seemed awfully frisky to her, tossing his head and cocking one ear back toward her. Somehow they'd talked her into spending the day and going for a ride.

"He'll calm down once we start climbing," Ty said behind her.

The three of them were going into the mountains. The idea was to reach some waterfall and have a picnic. She hoped it wouldn't take too long. Already, her rear was protesting the hardness of the saddle. The sheepskin saddle blanket should go on top of the darned thing. She needed the padding more than the horse.

When she glanced over her shoulder, Ty gave her a wicked grin. The rat! He knew what she was going through.

She faced the front and mused on why he'd agreed to the trip when the child had suggested it. Shane had urged her to accept the invitation. "The view is worth it," he'd told her with a twinkle in his eyes. She couldn't figure him out. It was almost as if he were pushing her and Ty together.

Squirming on the hard leather, she sent mental daggers his way. However, honesty forced her to admit she'd wanted to come and had jumped at the chance to spend the day with Ty and his son.

"Here's where the trail gets hard," Jonathan advised.

"Do tell," she murmured.

Behind her, she heard a quiet chuckle, then she didn't have time to attend to anything but staying in her seat as the gelding perkily lunged over a fat, squat boulder on the path. She grabbed the saddle horn and held on.

"Pull him in a bit," Ty advised. "Tighten the reins."

She gathered the leather straps more securely in her hand the way he'd shown her to hold them. Both he and Jonathan had been amazed that she'd never ridden a horse.

"It may come as a surprise, but I'd venture to guess that the great majority of people in

America haven't ridden a horse,'' she'd informed them when they'd commented on her deprived childhood.

''A person who can milk a cow can ride a horse,'' Ty had assured her. ''I have great confidence in you.''

''Famous last words,'' she muttered now to herself. She tried to move from the waist as he'd told her and keep her shoulders level. It wasn't as easy as he'd made it sound.

They moved on up into the hills, the trail wrapping around the slope and climbing higher and higher. The horses plodded along, puffing with the effort of walking uphill. She began to relax.

Everything was fine while they were in the trees. It was when they came out on a cliff that she nearly had a heart attack.

''Look, that's our house way down there.'' Jonathan pointed.

She peered over the edge and swallowed hard. It was a long way down.

Her horse was interested, too. He swung his head over the cliff and stared into the valley like John Muir discovering Yosemite. He took a step closer to the drop-off. Was he nearsighted or something? she wondered rather desperately.

"Whoa," she said. She pulled back on the reins.

The gelding tossed his head and pranced a bit.

"Easy," Ty said. He came up beside her, caught the reins in his big hand and held them firmly. "Easy, now. Relax."

She realized he was talking to her. Her temper flared. "It's the horse that needs talking to, not me."

Ty grinned. "The horse knows what he's doing."

"Meaning I don't?" She glared at him.

He chuckled. Jonathan gave her a big, encouraging smile. "Don't be afraid. Bandit's been up here lots of times."

Ty let go the reins and laid his hand on her leg. Heat ran through her thigh to her stomach. She darted a look at him.

His expression was sympathetic, his manner gentle. "It'll be worth the ride, once we get to the waterfall."

The tension rolled right out of her. "I'll let

you know about that when we get back home,'' she informed him.

When they moved on, she didn't worry about the long drop to her right. However, she did keep her eyes to the front.

A short time after that, they turned off the trail and entered a small glen. Water tumbled out of a rock face from several points and formed a tiny creek that rushed headlong down the mountain.

She dismounted when the two males did. Strong hands were suddenly there to hold her weight when she slid to the ground. It was a good thing. She found her legs were shaky.

''You'll get used to it,'' Ty said.

''Yeah, it takes a while, but you'll toughen up,'' Jonathan said with the voice of experience.

Ty removed the saddle, spread the blanket on the ground, using the saddle as a backrest. ''The seat of honor.'' He gestured for her to be seated.

She sank down gratefully. Ty had taken her home long enough to change into jeans and a blue T-shirt. She wore a long-sleeved shirt tied by the sleeves over her shoulders. She also had on her ragged sneakers and a hat.

"This is really lovely," she admitted while they ate peanut-butter-and-jelly sandwiches and drank warm lemonade from cans.

"Worth the trip?" Ty asked.

"Yes." Her gaze met his and lingered. She wondered why he'd seconded Jonathan's request that she come with them. It was almost as if he were testing her, seeing if she could fit into their life.

A nervous thrill went over her, and she looked away. She liked the ranch. Her time in the area had convinced her she could run a successful business there. She could be happy....

She looked around at Ty to give him a radiant smile, but he was studying the valley, which could be seen beyond the thin trunks of the evergreen trees hugging the side of the mountain. He looked troubled. She wondered what he was thinking.

It came to her that he must have been like Jonathan at one time, eager for adventure, a smile on his face as he rushed through the days, his heart open in trust and friendship.

Like her, he'd learned to be more cautious in his approach to life. So would Jonathan. With time. With heartbreak.

After polishing off her meal with an apple, she settled back on the saddle and closed her eyes. She heard Ty and Jonathan move off, their voices quiet as they explored the waterfall and creek.

When they returned, it was time for the trip home. Ty woke her with a tug on her hair. He had the other two horses saddled.

When they reached the meadow, Jonathan raced ahead of them. Ty let his horse mosey alongside hers. "Did you have fun?"

"Yes. It was wonderful."

"Good," he said in deepened tones.

She knew he was thinking of last night, as well as today. So much had changed between them in the past twelve hours, but she wasn't sure what any of it meant.

Or what she wanted it to mean. Falling in love wasn't in her work plan.

"Here, let me help you with that," Carly volunteered. She took the platter from Tina and carried it to the table.

"Thanks. That should do it. We can call the fellows now."

Carly went to the door and told the three blond-haired, blue-eyed males that the fish dinner was ready. When they trooped into the dining room, she felt an overwhelming surge of emotion. She turned back to the table to hide the tender feelings while the men went to other parts of the house to wash up.

Tina was watching her with an odd little smile on her face. When she realized Carly was looking at her, her smile widened. "Let's sit. I'm tired."

"Perhaps this was too much, cooking for extra people."

"Shane would have been crushed if we hadn't had the fish fry tonight. Besides, I love fresh fish. It's one of my favorite foods. Oh, put the pitcher of tea on the table, would you, please?" Tina took a chair at the end of the table.

Carly was worried about the other woman. Her hostess had caught her breath sharply several times while they prepared the meal. Once she'd had to stop and press her hands to her back.

"False labor," she'd explained. "It's nothing."

Carly hoped that was true. If the baby came that night and the fog crept up the river the way it had the previous night, Shane might have a hard time getting his wife to the hospital.

The three Macklin males came to the table. Carly poured tea for the adults and lemonade for Jonathan. Ty passed the platter of fish and hush puppies, which were fritters made with corn meal, a Southern dish that Tina had prepared from a recipe given to her by Genny Barrett. Tina had let Carly have the recipe, too.

Friends were like ripples in a pond, Carly mused while she ate. Each one touched another, which touched another and another and so on down the line. New ripples formed, their circles overlapping those of other ripples until everything was connected.

Glancing from one to another, she felt their lives touching hers and knew she'd like to be a part of them. Listening to Shane and Ty talk, she realized there was a close bond between the brothers that extended to Jonathan.

Both men listened to the boy tell his aunt of

the day's adventures. "We showed Carly how to clean her horse. She got horse hair in her nose and sneezed and sneezed. Then Dad and I fished in the river. That's how we got two more fish for dinner." He beamed with pride.

Carly felt a tightening in her chest. It would be so easy to get drawn into this family. They were warm and loving. Even Ty was relaxed in a way she'd never before seen.

Once in a while, their eyes met, and she felt the questions that neither had dared ask fill the air between them. Sometimes, his arm brushed hers, and she would feel all the wonder she'd felt during the night, of being able to snuggle close and touch him to her heart's content.

When Tina insisted they go to the family room for dessert rather than clearing the table, Ty caught Carly's hand and tugged her along to the other room. Then he, Shane and Jonathan went back to clean up the dishes and serve the banana pudding.

"I haven't seen Ty so relaxed in ages," Tina remarked when they were alone.

"It was a fun day." She grinned ruefully. "I may have overdone it a little with the horseback riding."

Tina gave her sympathetic smile. "You're good for Ty."

Carly didn't know what to say to that.

"You don't pander to his ego or seem to want him for his name or money."

Carly's head snapped up. "Of course I don't!"

Tina reached over and patted her hand. "Don't let his manner put you off. The Macklin men are the most hardheaded creatures I've ever met. Once they get an idea, they just don't let go. Shane was sure I came back here just to nab Ty when his marriage was falling apart." She laughed softly. "Which just goes to show how far wrong a person can be."

"Right," Carly agreed. "Obviously, you came back to nab *him*."

They laughed together. Tina caught her breath again and laid a hand on her tummy. "Quiet in there, buster," she muttered when she breathed easy once more.

"You're making me nervous," Carly told her. "How do you know these aren't the real thing?"

"Well, I don't, but unless something else happens, I'm going to assume all is well."

Carly held her breath when Tina gave a little gasp and bent forward a bit. "After we boil the water, what do we do?" she asked, keeping her tone light.

"I think Shane and Ty know. They've both had paramedic training as part of the sheriff's department."

"Ty is part of the department?"

"He's a volunteer deputy. In case of a disaster or unusual emergency," Tina explained. She bent forward again. "Oh," she said in a thin moan. "Getting harder."

Carly rose. "What is? Your pains? What should I do?"

Tina relaxed with a sigh. "Nothing. I'm fine."

When Ty came out with five plates and spoons, she gave him a worried frown and tried to warn him with her eyes to notice Tina.

He frowned and watched her warily as he put the plates down. "You okay?" he asked.

"Yes."

Couldn't he see that something was happening to Tina? The mother-to-be was bent over again, her hands braced on her knees, her head hanging forward as if she were studying the threads of the carpet.

Shane entered with Jonathan. The man had a big bowl of banana pudding. Jonathan carried the serving spoon.

The treat was eaten in near-silence as they listened to the muted sounds of evening. Carly suppressed a yawn. It was too peaceful. She was going to fall asleep.

"What's wrong?" Shane's deep voice broke the quiet.

Jonathan, Ty and Carly looked at him. His gaze was on his wife. They all looked at Tina. She had her teeth clamped into her lower lip and was bracing herself again.

"I think...it's for real this time," she said.

Shane jumped to his feet. "Let's go to the hospital."

"Not yet. It's far too early." Tina laughed as she relaxed, the sound reassuring to the others.

"Are you gonna have the baby, Aunt Tina?" Jonathan demanded.

"Maybe. We'll have to wait and see."

"I think I'd better go home—" Carly started.

"Ty," Shane broke in, bending over his wife. "I think we need to head for town. Can you drive? I'll stay in the back with Tina."

Ty exchanged a glance with his brother. "Sure. You want to use the pickup? The camper shell is on, so she can lie down on the cot if she needs to."

"Yeah. Let's do that." Shane disappeared.

Ty touched Carly's shoulder. "Would you drive Jonathan home and stay with him until I get back? He knows his routine, so you don't have to get him ready for bed. Do you mind?"

"No, of course not. Don't worry about us."

He handed her his car keys and headed out the door. In a minute, he was backing a pickup truck to the door. He blew the horn. Shane came through, Tina in his arms. She had her face pressed to his neck.

"Her water broke," he said. "The pains are a minute apart."

Carly held the door while he carefully stepped down to the patio. Jonathan came and stood beside her.

"Is she gonna have the baby?" he asked.

"It looks that way," Carly said.

"Wow, neat!"

Tina looked over Shane's shoulder as he lifted her into the back of the truck. "Maybe it'll be a boy cousin for you to play with," she called out, smiling gaily.

Carly felt a little weak. Along the river, the fog was gathering like an ensemble of ragged spirits. She and Jonathan watched until the truck disappeared.

"Well, I suppose we'd better get along to your house. It will be completely dark soon." She felt a shiver race along her arms.

"Yeah. We can tell ghost stories while we wait for Dad. Do you know any good ones?"

"No, but I'll listen to yours if you'll hold my hand."

"Okay." They went outside.

"Should we lock the door?" she asked.

He looked surprised. "I don't think so. What if Uncle Shane and Aunt Tina come home?"

"Don't they have a key?"

He shrugged. "Come on. Let's go."

She grabbed her purse and headed for Ty's truck. She drove very carefully over the county road while the fog gathered in the low areas. Jonathan directed her along the back road. She breathed a sigh of relief when they were safely home.

"Are you afraid of the dark?" Jonathan asked. He turned on the light in his room and got his pajamas from a drawer.

"No. The fog bothers me some, though. I didn't like driving in it."

He nodded in understanding. "When I was little, I used to be afraid of the wind. Dad said that was all right. The wind could be danger-ous. He showed me what to do in a storm. So now I'm not afraid anymore."

Carly wished someone would tell her what to do about her feelings for Ty, then maybe she wouldn't have to be afraid, either. "Shall I turn on the water for your shower?"

"Please. Then will you read to me?" His smile was endearing, just like his father's.

"How can I refuse?" she asked with a fa-talistic smile. It was too late to worry about the future. She'd already fallen in love with the father and the son. What more could go wrong?

Chapter Ten

Midnight had come and gone by the time Ty parked the truck beside the house and climbed out. He stretched wearily, then paused, looking at the house. The windows glowed softly with a welcoming light. His heart quickened.

He paused to reflect on the sensation. It worried him—this pull toward a woman, toward loving. It seemed to him that, as a man, he shouldn't need anyone. A man had to be self-sufficient.

So why the pull toward her? And the feeling that his life wouldn't be complete until she had a permanent place in it?

He entered the back door quietly. Going into

the hall, he glanced up the steps to the bedroom area, then headed toward the light shining from his study.

Carly was in there, curled up on the leather
sofa, sound asleep. The television was on, the
sound so low he could barely hear the talk-
show host deliver his one-liners.

A pang of longing hit him square in the
chest. He wanted to lift her in his arms and
carry her to his bed—

No.

He was already too deeply involved with
her. He wouldn't allow her to become necessary in his life. He'd been doing fine before
she came along. He'd do fine when she was
gone.

A picture of her at the ranch came to him.
Martha had indicated she missed the girl, as
she called her. They all did. Carly's manner
had been warm and admiring. She'd been interested in the ranch hands as people, not just
objects of curiosity to tell her friends about.

A heavy sigh escaped him. He wondered
what to do about her. His body immediately
supplied an answer.

Taking her to his bedroom and never letting

her go was not the thing to do, he told himself savagely, angry that he couldn't control the longing she induced.

Well, he'd better get her to bed. It had been a hell of a night, and it wasn't over yet. He walked across the braided rug, intending to shake her awake and tell her to use the guest room again. Her eyes opened when he stopped beside her.

She gazed up at him sleepily while her mouth widened in a welcoming smile. Like the lighted windows, it did something to his insides to know she'd waited up for him.

"How is Tina? And the baby?" A worried frown replaced the smile. "Are they all right?"

His intentions forgotten, he sat beside her, hip to hip, and brushed the strands of hair back from her temple. "Tina's fine. The baby's in intensive care. He's being checked out, but the doctor says he has a good chance of making it."

"I hope so," Carly murmured, her dark eyes so full of sympathy, it caused another lurch in the vicinity of his heart. "So it's a boy?"

"Yeah. A little over five pounds."

"Having babies...it still seems rather precarious even in this age of modern medicine, doesn't it?"

He let his hand drop to her shoulder. Through the T-shirt, he could feel the warmth of her body. It crept up his arm, reaching out and enclosing him in the sweet, wild tempest they'd shared the previous night at this time.

The witching hour.

"You bind me in your spell, river witch." He smiled at the whimsy, yet she called to him as only an enchantress could.

"No more than you do me."

He'd never met such a candid woman. He shook his head to clear the images of last night from his mind. There were practical things to consider. "Shane is staying at the hospital with Tina and the baby. I could see if Martha can come over here."

She looked confused. "Why?"

"To stay with Jonathan while I take you home." He looked out the window at the dense fog that had collected over the valley. "Or you can spend the night, and I'll take you home in the morning."

Her gaze followed his. He saw goose bumps

form on her arm as she viewed the fog. "I'll stay here."

"Good." His voice dropped to a husky register he couldn't control or disguise.

She looked at him, her eyes acknowledging the tension that was growing by the minute. "It's late. We'd better go to bed—" She stopped and waited, obviously uncertain where she was to sleep.

He closed his eyes and fought with the intense longing, but it was no good. There was no way he could let her go to bed alone. Not after last night.

Slipping his arms under her, he lifted her easily, her weight no burden at all. She nestled against his chest with a happy sound like the soft sigh of a kitten snuggling down.

Without thinking more on it, he carried her down the hall to his room. There, he set her on her feet and closed the door, pushing the lock into place to assure them of privacy.

"Jonathan—"

"Sleeps like a log," he interrupted.

She smiled slightly. "Is very well behaved, I was going to say. I like him."

"He likes you, too." Ty ran a hand through

his hair. He'd been tired when he got home, but now his body hummed with energy like an electric wire. "This doesn't mean anything," he warned her, determined to be fair.

"I know."

The words were spoken quietly, but there were undercurrents of emotion in them. She knew he was lying. So did he.

With sudden ruthlessness, he cupped her face between his hands. "I won't let it."

She returned his gaze without blinking. He held himself still as equal parts rage and desire built in him. He hadn't meant to let himself need her, to think of last night as anything more than a mutual satisfying of natural hunger.

It didn't work.

The long hours at the hospital had given him plenty of time to think. All his thoughts had revolved around their activities during the day and the long hours they'd spent together with his family. During dinner at Shane's house, he'd found himself thinking about him and Carly and Jonathan being together all the time. The scary thing was it didn't seem like such a crazy idea.

He slipped one hand behind her head and tugged gently. She rose on her tiptoes to accommodate the kiss. Her hands clutched his shoulders, and he sensed the shudder that went through her slender frame.

It came to him that she, too, was caught by their unexpected passion. Then he lost all ability to analyze as he became absorbed in the moment.

"Sweet," he murmured against her mouth. "The sweetest lips I've ever known."

He circled her waist with his hands and lifted her to him. She locked her ankles behind his back. He was swamped by warring feelings, but the one that stood out from the others was the sense of rightness. He was taken with the notion that this maddening, forthright female was *his*.

Carly knocked on the door of Isa's apartment, the feel of Ty's kisses still on her lips. It had been a strange, busy weekend.

Isa opened the door. "Carly, hello. About time you showed up. I expected you to drop by yesterday."

"I've been..." She couldn't think of a proper word.

Isa peered into her face. "Yeah, I can see you have. How about a cup of coffee? I think we need to have a serious talk."

They went inside. While Isa made coffee and toast, Carly fidgeted with her hair, replacing the barrettes in the sides. She put on lipstick and stared at herself in the tiny mirror on the side of the tube. She didn't look different, but she felt it.

She glanced about the small, neat apartment. It seemed a lifetime since she'd stayed there while on her way to a new life.

"Ty Macklin," Isa announced the topic of their talk.

"Yes." There didn't seem anything else to add to that.

"I tried calling your place. I assume you spent the weekend with him at his house?"

"Yes. Sort of." She explained about the fog and the accident on the highway, then about the baby. "A little boy. He's going to be okay. Shane called this morning to tell us before Jonathan left for school."

Isa groaned. "It's too late. You're already

head over heels, not to mention totally sucked in by this family.''

Carly grimaced at her friend, then sipped the coffee. ''I know. I've decided what I'm going to do.''

''What?''

''Take one day at a time.''

''You? The person who used to make five-year plans and revise them every month? How long will you be content with this one-day-at-a-time stuff?''

''I don't know. Do you think I should demand marriage?'' She laughed. ''I'm not sure I want the obligations that go with it. I have a new business to run. I should concentrate on that.''

Isa's expression took on a nostalgic air. ''Remember how we were going to be rich and famous and have perfect marriages along with perfect children and live next door to each other?''

''Well, we'll live near each other as soon as I can get permanently settled. One out of five isn't total failure.''

''Do you ever get tired of what you're doing?''

"No, I love it." She studied her friend.
"What's wrong?"

Isa shrugged in her graceful way. "I'm
tired, I think. I'm worried about my brother.
He's running around with a boy I don't like.
I'm not sure what to do. When I talk to him,
he tells me there's no problem."

"How are his grades? Are they dropping?
That's usually a clue. He may be cutting
classes."

"He's smart. He can make A's without
opening a book."

"When I move closer, maybe I can help."

"There's an empty apartment in this complex. If you moved up here, you could check
on Rick. He's supposed to be home and studying by nine, but I think he's getting in just
before I get home from the theater. What's he
doing out until midnight in a town like this?
They roll up the sidewalks on weekday
nights."

"You know I'll do anything I can to help."
Carly glanced at the clock, then hugged her
friend and hurried off to meet a supplier of
greeting cards. Her life was picking up speed
as the time drew near for her to open. That

would leave less time for involvement with local ranchers.

Thinking about Isa's problem, she remembered reading a story about lonely youngsters...latchkey kids, they were called. Isa had been one, as had her brother. Their father hadn't been very dependable. A schemer and dreamer, Isa had once described him.

Her mind drifted to Ty. Now, there was a father who took his responsibilities seriously. He'd even tutored the child at home so he wouldn't fall behind in school. These days, when the bus let Jonathan off at the end of the driveway, Ty was there to meet him. On the walk to the house, their avid discussions ranged over many topics.

Jonathan thought his father was great. He'd told her so after their bedtime story Saturday night. She thought so, too.

Ty drove the truck along the gravel road, annoyance niggling at the edges of his mind. Rodrigo had missed a fungus infection on the pasture near the river. Now it had spread to a neighboring field. They were going to try a new chemical spray since the disease had proved resistant to the methods they usually used.

The problem with Rodrigo was that he'd discovered Alys. Or vise versa. Now the horticulturist, whose job was to keep an eagle eye on the land and head off trouble, hung around the office most of the time on some pretext or the other.

And the girl…now, there was a study in feminine wiles. She fluttered her eyelashes so much she looked as if she were sending messages in Morse code. Hell, maybe she was.

A reluctant grin pulled at the corners of his mouth. It was for sure the couple didn't talk much. They just looked at each other, as moony eyed as poleaxed steers. Last Wednesday, he'd walked in to find them kissing. That had been the last straw.

He'd told them the office was a place of business and if Alys wanted to open a brothel to do it on her own time, not his. In response, Rodrigo had stuck his fists up in the air and demanded Ty step outside. Then Martha had appeared, angrier than he'd ever seen her, and ordered Alys home and told him to dock the girl's pay.

Of course, Alys had burst into tears, and Rodrigo had taken her off in his truck to comfort her. The upshot of all this drama was that the couple was planning a wedding, probably Christmas, Alys had confided with a giggle this morning. If they could wait that long.

God, had he ever been that young?

Remembering his experience with his former wife, he admitted he had. He'd thought he had to have her, that he couldn't live without her. He'd learned he could.

Yeah, the hard way, he mocked the memory.

Another memory embedded itself in his mind and wouldn't let go. Carly Lightfoot. It had been a week since he'd dropped her off at her place early Monday morning. He hadn't called or tried to see her since.

Jonathan had asked every morning if she was going to come back to spend the weekend with them. "I really like her, Dad."

He'd put the boy off. They'd spent the weekend with Shane and Tina. Jonathan had been fascinated with the new baby. On the way home, he'd confided he would *really* like to have a brother.

Ty sighed. He got out of the truck and

hefted the sprayer over the tailgate. Holding the nozzle in one hand, he directed the spray over the affected area. Life would be easier, he thought, if a person could blot out emotions with a quick soaking of some miracle medicine.

A harsh tightening inside told him how much he wanted to see Carly again. And therein lay the danger. She was smart, ambitious, dedicated to her work. She obviously didn't need him.

Maybe that was part of her allure. She looked at him in wonder, with no guile that he could detect in the direct gaze from those dark eyes. Maybe he'd been wrong to suspect her motives. Sure, she'd come there on a whim, but that had nothing to do with the attraction between them.

He finished the task and climbed back in the pickup. Turning, he drove along the river path instead of the dusty gravel road.

When he rounded a bend along the meandering water, he stopped in surprise. Ahead of him, next to the weeping willow, Carly stood, talking with Venita.

The young wrangler shook her head and

backed off. Carly spoke more urgently. He gripped the steering wheel in fury. What the hell was she up to?

Carly sighed as Venita hurried away. There had been a scene in town between Pete Hodkin and a waitress at Smitty's. Carly wanted Venita to testify to the police that the brute had also accosted her so that they could build a case against him, but the girl was frightened of the man.

Her attention was caught by a movement at the corner of her eye. She whipped around. Ty was a hundred feet away.

He didn't look too happy to see her. She stuck her hands on her hips and waited while he drove closer.

"What are you doing here?" he asked as soon as he killed the engine and threw open the door. He swung his long legs to the ground and stalked toward her. He stuck his hands on his hips as if parodying her stance and glared at her.

"Well, I was trying to get Venita to go with me to report the assault by Hodkin that time, but she doesn't want to get involved." She frowned in disgust. "That's why bullies like him are still on the street. People are afraid to speak up." She explained about the contretemps at the restaurant.

He heaved an exasperated breath as worry for her crusading efforts cut through him. "You're going to get yourself in trouble if you don't quit butting into other people's business. What about your promise?"

She stared at him blankly. "What promise?"

"Uh-huh," he said as if her failure to know what he was talking about confirmed some suspicion he'd had for a long time.

"I didn't make any promises."

"You said you'd watch out for Hodkin and stay out of his way. The man could be dangerous."

"That's why he should be locked up. He got fresh with the waitress. When she told him to keep his hands to himself, he hit her right across the face."

She looked so indignant while she related this that Ty had to grip his arms tightly to his body to keep from hauling her into them and taking her home to keep her safe. He frowned at her instead. "Were you there?"

"Of course not. The waitress is my neighbor. She lives in the next apartment. I saw the bruise on her cheek—"

"And just had to butt in."

"Naturally, I asked her about it. She came home early Saturday and had obviously been crying. I'd just got in with some groceries and had her over for coffee. I could hardly ignore her."

"Of course not," he remarked sarcastically. "Have you confronted Hodkin yet with his misdeeds?"

"No. I went to Sheriff Keeler this morning. By the way, your brother was at the county office, too. It seems they've been having another string of thefts up his way. Hodkin is suspected. I told them I'd check into Hodkin on this end—"

Ty took her by the arm and hauled her toward the truck. "I'll have Keeler's ears pinned to the barn door for this. Shane's, too."

She climbed inside, then asked with an eager smile, "How's the baby? Is he home yet?"

He felt an odd pang go through him. He

softened his manner a fraction. "They brought Ian home Wednesday. He's doing fine."

"Good. I was worried—"

She was startled into silence when he slid into the truck and pushed over beside her, his hip and thigh pressing against hers as he rooted her over. He was immediately aware of her, of the heat that flowed between them where they touched, of the pure animal magnetism that existed between them.

She went very still.

When he dared look at her, he saw the same awareness in her eyes. Flames leapt between them, engulfing them in the hunger neither wanted to acknowledge.

A heavy sigh escaped him. "Oh, hell," he said.

He was defeated by her smile, her closeness, her courage. A week apart had only increased the need. He gave up.

Carly saw the flames leap into his eyes and felt her own resolutions shatter.

Men burn and women yearn.

Why this man? she thought, perplexed by feelings she had no control over whatsoever. Why him and no other?

He caught a handful of her hair and made a fist. ''I see you and all my sane and sensible ideas go winging off, never to be seen again.'' He laughed ruefully. ''Well, what happens next?''

''I don't know.''

''Don't you? I thought women always had all the answers. If you were like other women, we'd be talking marriage by now.'' He let her go and ran a hand through his own thick hair.

She realized he looked tired, as if he hadn't slept any better than she had that week. Well, that was some compensation. At least she wasn't suffering alone.

''Ty, I'm sorry,'' she said softly. ''I know I shouldn't have come here. Venita called me. She's worried about one of the cowhands who works for you, but she wouldn't tell me his name. She thinks he's involved with Hodkin. She wouldn't admit anything over the phone. That's why I came here to see her in person. It all sort of ties together, don't you see?''

''Did you find out who the man was?''

''No, she still wouldn't say. She's afraid she'll get him in trouble with...whoever.''

Carly shrugged despondently. "I want to help, but I can't without her cooperation."

"I'll see what I can do," he said slowly, thinking it over.

"Do you think she would talk to you?"

He shook his head. "But Martha might."

"Oh, yes. That may work. Martha seems to know everything." She smiled up at him, glad that he'd thought of something. Her words of gratitude dried up in her throat when she met his eyes. His gaze burned hotly over her face, settling on her lips. She licked them self-consciously.

"Don't do that," he murmured in a low growl.

"What?"

"Look like that...as if the world were full of wonder...as if I were the cause of it."

"I think you are," she admitted, and sighed helplessly. "When you touch me, everything seems to glow."

He made an inarticulate sound, then stared straight ahead. The angle of his jaw seemed to be set in concrete as he fought the demon of their mutual desire.

"This has been some week," he finally said.

"I forgot to write down two shipping dates. The trucks arrived for the cows, and we weren't ready. I put checks in the wrong envelopes. I couldn't get my bank account to balance...." He let the complaints die away and stared into space.

"I forgot an appointment with a vendor. I wore the jacket to one outfit and the skirt to another. I couldn't remember the name of my store when somebody asked," she recounted her misfortunes.

"I haven't slept." He faced her. "That's why I don't want you here. Seeing you makes me remember—" He stopped abruptly.

"Weekend before last?" she taunted, and was vengefully delighted to see him flinch.

"That was a low blow," he muttered, his eyes narrowing.

"You deserved it. Men act like it's the woman's fault that they can't sleep or concentrate or anything—"

"Can you?" he broke in harshly, his face suddenly close to hers as he stared into her eyes. "Can you sleep and not remember the nights in my arms and how good it was?"

"No," she stated with utmost truthfulness.

She cast him a resentful glance. "I need to go. It's obvious I'm not going to get anything done here today."

"Have you talked to Rodrigo? He may know something. Or Alys."

"The Lolita from your office? Why would she know anything?"

Ty grinned. "She's engaged to Rodrigo."

"You're putting me on." When he shook his head, she rolled her eyes to heaven. "I thought he had more sense than that."

"Apparently not. You women work your spells, and we men are the ones who pay the piper."

"Oh, you poor dears. It must seem terribly unfair. After all, men have been calling the tune for centuries. It must be terrible to have to move over and let others share the power."

A snort of laughter burst from him at her facetious manner. "I don't think we ever had any power. It was, alas, but an illusion." He laid a hand over his heart.

She gazed at him in exaggerated worry. "We'd better go before the bull manure gets any higher."

With a snort of laughter, he started the truck

and wound along the river path until they turned toward the ranch buildings. He parked in the shade of a shed.

She waved to William, who stood outside the barn smoking a cigarette. Ty glanced from the young man to her. "Another of your conquests."

"Hardly. I've only spoken to him a couple of times."

"I saw him in your car."

"One time. I gave him a ride to town." She laid a hand on Ty's arm. "He sat at a table with Pete Hodkin and some others. I watched them in my rearview mirror. They were having a pretty heavy discussion about something. I wish I could have heard them."

Ty frowned. "That inquisitive little mind of yours is going to get you into trouble one of these days."

She batted her eyelashes prettily. "You'll rescue me like you did before, won't you?"

"I don't know. I might let you sink or swim on your own." His gaze went to her lips and lingered. His face hardened when he saw her watching him with knowing laughter in her eyes. He reached for the door handle.

She said nothing, but climbed out of the truck when he did and walked to her car.

"Do you want to have dinner Saturday night?" he asked.

Stopping with her hand on the handle of the car door, she studied his expression carefully. "Excuse me? For a minute there, I thought you asked me to dinner."

He scowled. "I did."

"Well," she said. She'd dreamed of doing things with him and his son for a week. Now that the invitation had come, she knew she couldn't.

"Jonathan thought you might like another riding lesson, then we'll grill some hot dogs."

She opened the car door and slipped inside, then paused after putting the key in the ignition switch. "Tell Jonathan I said thanks, but I really have a lot of work to do. The shop will be opening in mid-December for the Christmas holidays. I have to pick out carpet and shelving before then."

Ty actually looked relieved. "Well, then," he said, "we'll see you around." He closed the car door.

She rolled down the window. "Ty, be careful. If someone here is working with Hodkin, they could be planning on stealing something from the ranch. Shane said they mostly took tractors and equipment like that.''

''I'll keep an eye out for trouble here.''

She nodded.

He stepped back so she could leave.

It was time to go. She cranked up the engine and put the car in reverse. After giving him one more glance, she backed up, then pulled out on the driveway and headed for the highway. He watched her until she was out of sight.

She watched him, too.

Ty parked the pickup next to the house, too tired to put it in the garage. He'd worked hard all day and was dog tired.

During the afternoon, a conveyor belt had broken. They'd had to move hay by hand. Then he'd had to drive up to Medford for a part, then had spent another hour fixing the problem. That had thrown him hours late in finishing. It was after seven. He'd been on the go since five that morning.

In the house, he headed for a shower, dropping clothes over the bedroom floor as he went, then picking them up and sticking them in the hamper. His mother hadn't allowed the boys to be slobs while they were growing up. He found it hard to be one now.

Funny, the things that lingered with a man.

He thought of Carly. When she'd been at the house, it had seemed filled with her cheery presence. His son had liked her. So had he. Too much.

Stepping into the shower, he turned the water on and recalled a sleek feminine form that had molded itself to him like a cat wanting to be stroked. She'd liked his touch.

He'd liked hers, too. Maybe the thing between them should be explored more fully.

No commitment, though. He wasn't thinking along those lines. He'd made a big mistake once before. He couldn't do that again. He had his son to think of now. He didn't want Jonathan to learn to depend on a woman and then *poof!* have her disappear.

Yeah, he'd be careful this time.

He got out of the shower and dressed in fresh jeans and a white shirt. Rolling the sleeves back, he thought of the evening ahead.

Jonathan was spending the night at his best friend's house and staying over for a birthday party tomorrow, so he was at loose ends. He could go over to Shane's house, but he figured they needed some privacy as a family to get used to the new baby.

After watching the evening news, he wondered if Carly was free. She was probably still working in her shop, which was the size of the walk-in closet in the bedroom.

Without giving himself time to reconsider, he called the store. She answered on the second ring.

"Is dinner a possibility?" he heard himself ask.

There was a lengthy pause. "I suppose so."

"Don't be so enthusiastic. I might get ideas."

She laughed. "I don't think you need encouragement along those lines."

"I'm bashful, don't you know?" He smiled as she laughed again, that husky gurgle that reminded him of secret glens and bubbling brooks.

Minutes later, he was on his way. When he turned onto the county road that would take him to the resort, he wondered what the hell he was doing, then realized he didn't care. For the first time in years, he felt happy and care-free. He wasn't going to analyze the reasons why, not tonight.

Chapter Eleven

Carly was in the tiny shop when he arrived. "I'm almost through here," she said as he ducked under the security gate. She finished installing glass shelves in a corner cabinet.

He eyed her clothing. She wore a cherry red sweater-and-slacks outfit. Her hair was pulled to one side and held in place with a big white clip. Snowflake earrings shimmered with every movement of her head. She looked like a million.

He wanted to ease in behind her and nibble a bit on her neck while she looked over a pile of receipts and entered the numbers in her computer. "Shall we eat here?"

She flashed him a grateful smile. "That will be fine."

He realized she was tired. How many hours had she put in that day and the day before? "Don't you have anyone to help you?"

"With the decorating? No. I like doing my own thing."

"Yeah, you would." Tenderness washed over him.

When she finished with her work, she retrieved her purse and coat, then raised the metal gate so he didn't have to duck under, stepped outside with him, then lowered and locked it into place.

A sign on the wall proclaimed the shop to be The Cricket Cage. An apt name. Her hours would be from ten until six.

During dinner, they talked of their respective labors in almost desultory tones. Desire was kept to a low simmer by their mutual fatigue. Raging passion didn't have to dominate every moment, he discovered. Sharing the quiet was nice, too.

When a band began to play, they danced to the soft music, leaving the wilder stuff to the more energetic members of the crowd. When she yawned and then sighed, he realized it was time to call it a night.

He held her white cashmere coat while she slipped her arms into it. He realized she probably bought it, that she didn't need a man to do things for her. She could do them all herself.

The knowledge gave him an odd feeling, as if his one advantage had disappeared. Strange that he should feel that way.

Outside, she murmured, "I have my car," when he steered her toward his.

"I forgot." He walked her to it. The snow crunched under their feet. The November rains had produced snow on the mountain peaks around the valley. There was only a sliver of moon, and the valley far below was pitch-black. The setting took on a surreal glow, reminding him of onyx surrounded by diamonds.

They stood in the parking lot, neither speaking. He didn't quite know what to say. He only knew what he wanted—for her to come home with him...without question, without hesitation, without arguing the sense of it...just come.

"My house is closer," he said.

She shook her head. "I've taken a room in a nearby bed-and-breakfast inn. I'm looking for a house to buy."

"Oh." He swallowed against the words that lodged in his throat. He wasn't even sure what they were. God, he was thirty-five. He should be past this adolescent uncertainty.

She unlocked the car door and put her hand on the handle.

"I thought maybe you'd like to stay with me."

"Are you asking me to spend the night?"

"Yes." It was hard to say. It felt like a commitment, or the start of one. Hell, he didn't know. Maybe it was.

She was silent for so long he concluded she was going to say no and was trying to think of a polite way to do it. "All right."

"You will?"

Her laughter washed over him, gentle and teasing. "Yes. I was hoping you'd ask."

That set off so many sparks inside him, he wanted to take a room at the resort and stay there. "Lock your car and let's go."

"I have to work in the morning."

"I'll bring you in."

"It's too far. Why don't I follow you?"

"I want you with me." A simple confession, but filled with so many complications, he couldn't begin to name them.

"All right." She locked the car.

Just like that. No fuss. No arguments. Gratitude hit him. He wanted to worship at her feet. He really was going off the deep end. And he didn't care.

They drove to his place in silence with her sitting close like teenagers on a date. He draped an arm around her and drove with his left hand until he had to make the turn onto the ranch road, which required both hands. He could feel her breast against his arm. By the time they reached the house, he was uncomfortable in his jeans.

"What's that?" she asked.

He looked to where she pointed. A man was making his way along the paddock fence, clinging to it as if he'd fall if he let go. He was heading for the stable.

"It's William, isn't it?" She peered through the dark. "I think he's hurt."

They got out of the car together, but his longer stride brought him to the younger man quickest. "What's happened?" he asked, looping an arm around the cowhand's torso and swinging William's arm over his shoulders to take some of his weight.

"Had a little accident," William muttered through a swollen lip.

"Someone beat you up," Carly put in. "Who? Why?"

William attempted to laugh. It ended in a cough. "Nobody. Barroom brawl. Dumb to get…involved. Think I stove in a couple of ribs. I was going to get the liniment."

Ty guided him toward the bunkhouse kitchen. "Let's see how bad you're hurt. We might need to see the doc—"

"No doctor," William insisted, breathing with difficulty. "I'm okay."

"Right," Carly snapped sarcastically.

He grinned. "I've lived through worse."

Ty patched the man up with antiseptic, horse liniment and butterfly bandages to hold a busted lip until it healed. "You'd better not do any lifting for a few weeks."

"I can work."

"No, you can't. He can't," Carly appealed to Ty.

He nodded. "He can help with the paper-work. With the situation at the office, we need all the help we can get."

Carly suppressed a laugh. She knew he was thinking of Alys and Rodrigo. When he turned a sharp eye on her, she straightened up and tried to look solemn.

"Ready for bed?" Ty asked William.

William nodded.

"I'll be back. Wait here." Ty helped the cowboy limp into the other room, where only William and Rodrigo slept now that the other cowboys were gone. Soon Venita and William would also be gone for the winter. Venita was studying veterinary medicine. Carly didn't know what William did during the off-season.

When he was safely inside and in bed, Ty returned to her. They went outside and stood in the moonlight in the quadrangle between the office, the barn and stables and pasture.

A short way through the trees, his house stood like a ghostly sentinel, outlined in silver by the thin moonlight.

"How about something warm to drink?" Ty suggested, rubbing his arms as the chill seeped in.

"Sounds good. Don't you ever wear a coat?"

"It's in the truck. I'll hold you instead." He looped an arm around her and pulled her into his side. Hip to hip, they walked through the wooded path to his house.

They entered through the back door. Ty flipped on lights as they went inside.

"Where's Jonathan?" She looked around as if expecting the child to materialize out of thin air.

"Spending the night with a friend."

"Oh."

"Yeah," he said. "We're alone. I didn't plan it. Things just worked out this way."

"So you were at loose ends when you called me." She thought of the situation at his office and grinned.

"What?" he asked. He got out a pan, a container of milk, then bread and margarine. After putting on the chocolate to heat, he made cinnamon toast.

"I was thinking of Alys and Rodrigo. The office must be…"

"It is," he agreed when she broke off, not

sure how to describe the torrid atmosphere that probably existed between the young lovers.

"Serves you right for being such a cynic about love."

"What, catching them in a clench or having to watch them go all dumbstruck in each other's presence?" Ty heaved an exasperated sigh and shook his head. "It isn't safe to walk in the office. I make a lot of noise before I dare enter."

Laughing, Carly removed two mugs from the cabinet and poured cocoa for them. She set the table with napkins while Ty placed the toast slices on two plates.

They ate quickly, not talking much until they were finished. Ty stuck the dishes in the dishwasher, then they went into his study with their mugs.

"What do you think really happened to William?" she asked.

"Well, he was definitely in a fight, no question about that."

"I'll bet it was Hodkin and his friends who beat him up."

He gave her a speculative glance. "Aren't

you a bit prejudiced? You seem to think he's the cause of all bad things.''

"He usually is."

"I'll check it out," he promised. "Maybe William will tell me the story. It may have been a brawl, you know. They have them fairly regularly when the loggers and cowboys go into town.''

"I'm probably paranoid about the man, but thanks for looking into it. I knew you would." She beamed at him.

"Did you?" he asked quietly.

She returned his gaze levelly. "Yes."

He stood and came to her. Taking the mug from her, he placed it on the coffee table. When he held out a hand, she placed hers on his and rose at his gentle tug. He enclosed her in his arms.

"What am I going to do about you?" he asked. He laid his head on hers and seemed to ponder the question.

"Take me with a grain of salt?" she suggested, refusing to melt against him.

"I'll take you any way I can get you."

Lifting her, he placed her on the sofa and

lay beside her. She felt the quick rise and fall of his chest against hers.

"One day at a time, then," she told him, voicing her own philosophy regarding them.

"I'm a rancher. We have to plan ahead, season by season, for at least a year, usually longer." He kissed along her temple, following a meandering path to the corner of her mouth. "A week," he murmured. "That's too long."

"Yes." She ran her hands over his chest, then opened his shirt and slipped them inside, loving the pure sensuality of touching him.

"I want to look at you." He slipped his hands under her cotton knit sweater.

She sat up and let him take it off. Under it, she wore a teddy rather than her usual underclothes.

"Who did you wear this for?" he asked in thickened tones.

"The tooth fairy."

He chuckled softly, then became serious as he rubbed a knuckle over the silky material until her nipple stood out against it.

She closed her eyes when his lips moved down her throat. He pressed her into the cushions, then ravished her breasts until she moaned and writhed helplessly against him.

When he carried her up the steps and down the hall to his bedroom, she couldn't deny what her heart and body had known for ages. She was in love, foolishly, totally in love with this man.

They had waffles for breakfast. Ty made them while she sat on a bar stool and watched. She stretched, feeling as contented as a cat in the sun. Their lovemaking had been wild last night, gentle this morning.

When the meal was ready, she helped carry it to the table. Once seated, she took a bite and chewed thoughtfully, her gaze on the mountains that rose to the north of them.

Ty finished first. He stretched his long legs to the side and took a sip of coffee, his eyes on her. When he propped the mug on his abdomen, he continued his study.

''Do I have syrup on my chin?'' she at last asked, growing self-conscious under his scrutiny.

''No. You look beautiful.'' He smiled when she looked away. ''A woman who's embarrassed when she's paid a compliment,'' he mused. ''How extraordinary.''

She gave her head a little toss. ''I'm not embarrassed,'' she denied. ''I was merely wondering why you said it. I know perfectly well that I'm not beautiful.''

Finished with the meal, she gathered the dishes and cleaned up the kitchen. When she returned to the table, he hooked an arm around her waist and settled her on his lap.

''You are to me,'' he murmured. He ran one hand up and down her back as if to soothe her.

His gentleness caused an ache to start inside. She tried to ignore it and the yearning that stirred in her. It was foolish to attach any importance to words spoken in sexual gratification.

''Watch it,'' she warned. ''I might start to believe you, then I'd become vain and flirt like Alys—''

He groaned in dismay and cut her off with a kiss. At that moment, the back door opened. They whipped around.

''Ah, excuse me,'' Shane said. He came in and closed the door. Going to the counter, he poured a cup of coffee and joined them at the table.

"Make yourself at home," Ty suggested wryly.

Carly was seated in her own chair again by this time. She kept her gaze demurely on her hands, which were clasped around her coffee cup.

"Sorry. This is important. Sheriff Keeler was put out of action last night."

"Oh, no!" Carly leaned forward. "Is he... was he—?"

"Killed? No, nothing like that. He was whacked on the head pretty hard and is in the hospital for observation. He probably has a concussion. When he was hit, just before he passed out, he heard someone mention Carly as next on the list—"

Ty muttered a harsh curse.

"I checked your place at the resort. Your car was there, but you weren't. Bill said he saw you and Ty at dinner last night, so I traced you to here. I wanted to warn you to watch yourself."

"I'll see that she does," Ty volunteered.

Shane ignored him. His gaze was on Carly's

shocked face. "I think you should be extra-careful. Don't go anywhere alone."

"She'll be careful," Ty interjected. "She can stay here."

She gasped in astonishment. "I can't stay with you. I travel a lot, looking for gift ideas. It would interfere with my work."

He gave her a determined glare. "No, it won't. Things have slacked off here. I'll drive while you do your errands each day and bring you home when you're through. No one will hurt you." It was a promise.

It gave her a strange feeling, to know he was willing to protect her. "Your life could be in danger if I stay with you," she reminded him. "You have a son who needs you."

"Jonathan will be okay. So will I. And you. Bullies don't show themselves if there's a chance the odds aren't in their favor." His smile was definitely threatening toward anyone who hurt those who were under his care.

She glanced at the sheriff, who observed them without comment. There was a wealth of knowledge in his blue eyes, and she knew the situation between her and Ty was obvious to him. A blush started in her chest and went right to her hairline.

"What do you think I should do?" she asked him, desperate for a sensible reason why she couldn't stay here.

"Stay," he said. "It's a good idea. Ty can keep on eye on you after hours. You should be safe enough at the resort. I'll alert the resort security to watch things. I don't think Jonathan will be in danger, but he can stay at our place for a while."

"Good," Ty said as if it were all settled. "I'll take Jonathan to school each morning, then drop you off at work. I'll pick you up at night. You can stay here."

"No," she objected, her head swimming at the thought.

"That's an excellent plan," Shane confirmed. His eyes seemed to gleam with some secret amusement of his own. He drank down the rest of the coffee and rose. "I'm going over to talk to Keeler. I'll see if he can remember anything else."

"I'll ask around, too," Carly volunteered.

"The hell you will," Ty said with ominous quiet.

"If I'm going to be here, I may as well be useful. Venita might decide to talk—"

"No."

Shane grinned, tipped his head to them and left.

"I'll talk to the waitress." She gave Ty a defiant stare.

He glared at her for a long second, then smiled. "Now, where was I? Oh, yes, I was about to…"

He refilled their coffee mugs and came back for her. Lifting her in his arms, he finished the sentence. "I was about to kiss you senseless." He didn't give her time to think beyond that.

"And so I'm staying here for now," Carly finished up. She paused for comment, but there was silence on the other end of the line. "Brody?" she said to her foster brother.

"Let me speak to this guy Macklin," he said.

"Why?" she asked, alarmed by his tone. Brody was not known as a mincer of words.

"I want to ask him a few questions."

"Well, he's not at the house right now." Through the kitchen window, she could see Ty approaching at a fast clip. "Listen, I have to go. I'll talk to you later."

"Be careful," he ordered.

"I will. Bye for now." She hung up just as Ty walked in the back door.

He glanced at the telephone, then at her. "I'll take a quick shower, then we'll go."

"Fine. I'm ready."

He looked her over. "Pretty." He bounded up the stairs in two steps. In a minute, she heard the shower come on. Glancing at the calendar, she realized it was fast closing on Christmas. She wondered what the holiday would bring.

It had been a little over seven weeks since she'd arrived to start her new job as a cook's helper. At the time, she'd romanticized the idea of living on a ranch. Now she loved it, being here with Ty, watching the season slowly change, playing in the fallen leaves with his son, riding, laughing, loving...

It was almost as if they were married. Worse, she knew Jonathan wanted them to be. He was such a loving child.

She pondered the idea of marriage and sharing a lifetime with Ty. He was neat around the house. He made up the bed in his room each morning. He was protective but not smothering as she'd feared. He and Shane had decided she could drive herself to the resort, but Ty would go with her on shopping trips.

Standing at the window, she wondered if she could really be in danger. Sheriff Keeler thought she was. That was enough for the Macklin brothers. Bossy, protective men...

Her musing was interrupted by the sight of Martha and her niece heading for the ranch office. They were laughing and talking with great animation. A sense of isolation swept over her. She'd hardly seen Isa since she'd started on this venture. She missed her friend.

"Ready?"

Spinning around, she caught her breath at how incredibly handsome Ty was. In fresh navy slacks and a white shirt, he looked like every girl's dream of a hometown sweetheart—handsome, athletic and intelligent.

He crossed the room and tilted her chin up with one finger. "Keep looking at me like that," he warned huskily, "and you'll never get to your shop."

"Ha, so you've said before." She wrinkled

her nose at him and pushed him to arm's length.

Leading the way, she went out to the truck and climbed in. He joined her. Sliding one more glance over her that made every cell in her body hum with tension, he headed for the highway. After picking up an order from Elena, they went to the resort.

Ty went in with her and watched her open the gate. He wondered that she didn't feel claustrophobic in the tiny room, but it was clearly something she loved.

She smiled and murmured a soft goodbye. His cue to leave. Still he lingered, watching her go through a book of sample fabric swatches, holding various squares up to the finished wall.

Three teenage girls stopped by. They asked her about her store and looked at the items she'd selected for the grand opening.

One of them flirted boldly with him, which made him smile. Carly gave him an oblique glance. She was probably wondering what he was doing still hanging around.

She was friendly with the girls, but soon

sent them on their way, saying she had a ton of work to do. She handled it well.

For a moment, pride swelled his chest. As if she were his woman, he wanted to brag about her to other guys and point out that *this* female was his. It was a crazy notion.

But when she glanced his way, her eyes dark and rich with amusement and warmth, it seemed real.

He waved and left, wondering how he was going to control the mad impulses he got when they were together. That morning, on the way to school, Jonathan had asked him if Carly could live with them "for all time."

Ty had explained that she was visiting with them for a while.

"But are we gonna marry her? I'd like to, Dad. She's neat."

"That's something only grown-ups can decide," he'd said with a casualness he was far from feeling.

Jonathan had worried about the situation on the way to the elementary school in town. "You'll be nice to Carly, won't you? Sometimes you get mad and say things. I know you don't mean them, or not the way it sounds like you mean them, but she might not.''

''I'll watch my temper,'' he'd promised.

''Gee, I wish I hadn't promised Aunt Tina I'd help with the baby this week. I could explain to Carly about when you get mad.''

''It's all right, son. I can manage to be civil for a week.''

During the rest of the day, the situation between the three of them lingered in his mind. He wondered if he was as hard to live with as his son's worry had implied.

Well, he'd watch his temper and his tongue and try not to hurt his guest's feelings, which Jonathan had thought was a definite possibility when he'd left the boy at the school gate.

''Be careful, Dad, will you?'' he'd asked.

''Right. I'll weigh every word before I say it.''

''Good.''

That evening, playing a game of catch with Jonathan on Shane's lawn, he couldn't help but smile as he recalled his son's relief that he was going to try to act right and talk nice to Carly. The smile disappeared as he thought of how much Jonathan wanted Carly to live with them on a permanent basis. He'd fallen hard for her.

Like his old man had?

A lump settled in Ty's chest. He pulled into the parking lot at the resort and stayed in the truck, watching the skiers depart.

Was he in love with Carly Lightfoot?

That wasn't even the most important question, he realized. If his first wife hadn't been able to stand the life associated with being a rancher's wife, what chance would marriage have with a career-minded woman like Carly?

"She's good," Bill Johnson, the building manager, remarked, stopping beside Ty in the resort hallway.

"Yes, she is." Ty propped a shoulder against the cool surface of the wall and waited for her to finish with her last supplier.

"She has a good eye for merchandise. She could move up to a bigger store any time she wanted. She says she likes it fine right here and that her store is the perfect size. Her marketing niche, she called it." Bill shrugged, grinned, then hurried on as if late for an appointment.

The metal gate creaked as it lowered. Carly locked it, then turned to him, taking off her earrings as she did.

"Be with you in a minute," she told him. She hurried down the hall in the opposite direction.

He watched her appreciatively, liking the provocative sway of her hips under a knit skirt. She stopped by a doorway. A man, good-looking in a tough kind of way, came into the hall. He wore the uniform of a security guard for the resort.

Ty frowned as a tightness entered his chest. He wasn't jealous, not at all, but he didn't like the way the man's eyes roamed her figure while they talked. Once she laughed, and they both glanced down to where Ty stood waiting for her.

There was speculation in the guard's gaze. Ty smiled, realizing she must have told the guard she was leaving with him. The tight feeling dissipated.

Carly went into the ladies' room. She was back in a few minutes, dressed in jeans and her old sneakers.

They certainly were full of holes. He'd buy her a dozen pair of new ones when—

He broke the thought off before it could be completed. He wasn't thinking of a future with her. A man would be a fool to think a woman like her would stay in a backwater like this forever. She'd probably head back for the big city when she grew tired of the bucolic life.

Carly listened to the radio on the way to Ty's house, aware of him following at a safe distance behind her on the gravel back road. She'd worked hard that day and was utterly weary.

The resort was open from eight in the morning until midnight, but the stores closed earlier. She'd selected an eight-hour workday from ten until six. It was December 3. Opening day was only two weeks away if all went well.

At Ty's home, settled in the family room, she told him of her plans. "That will make it easier to protect me, won't it? I'll be in early— it'll hardly be dark—so you won't have to be running back and forth to the resort."

"I don't mind."

The light was blinking on the answering machine. He flicked the button and listened to his messages. One was from Shane. He wanted to see Ty and asked if he'd come over. Before he left, Ty reminded her to stay inside.

"I will," she promised.

He stopped beside her on the way to the back door. "I won't be gone long. We have to look over a contract."

She nodded. He leaned down to give her a kiss. She lifted her mouth to his. He slipped a hand along her cheek and into her hair, pulling her closer.

"God, you feel good."

Her eyes drifted closed as she savored his words. She luxuriated in the soft, urgent kisses he rained upon her face. These were the moments she held fast in her heart to remember when this time was past.

When he lifted his head, he stared into her eyes. There were questions in his, questions he would have to answer, not her. It reminded her of one of those featured articles in a magazine—"Can This Relationship Work?"

Neither of them knew the answer. She contemplated the situation after he left but was no nearer a solution when the phone rang sometime later.

Chapter Twelve

"Carly, can you meet me at the stable? I have something to tell you."

Chills crawled up Carly's neck at the urgent summons. The caller was Venita. "Can't you tell me on the phone?"

"No, I was told not to."

"All right," she said, making a quick decision. "I'll be there in a minute." She pulled a dark jacket on and removed a flashlight from the kitchen drawer. She'd use it as a weapon if needed.

Instead of going the most direct route—out the kitchen door and across the stable yard—she slipped out the front door and through the line of oak trees, across the road and along the paddock fence. She reached the corner of the stable without being accosted by anyone.

Venita waited in the shadows.

Carly stepped from behind the corner. "Venita?"

The girl started and clutched her hands against her chest. "Carly? Is that you?" she whispered.

"Yes. What's happening?"

"I wanted to warn you...there might be trouble here—"

"When? What kind of trouble?"

"I don't know, but you could be in danger. You mustn't go out alone, and you're to stay in the house if anything happens."

"Who told you this?"

Venita shook her head. "That's all I know."

"Who passed the warning to you to give to me?"

"It doesn't matter. Just...be careful."

"When is this *trouble* supposed to happen?"

"Soon, I think." The young cowgirl shivered. "I have to get back to the house. It's cold out here." She rushed off.

Carly watched until the door opened and closed behind Venita, then she made her way back to the main house over the same route she'd taken to leave it.

When Carly arrived at the house, she saw the light from the kitchen window shining on the driveway. Had she left it on? Or was Ty inside waiting for her?

He was waiting.

She'd hardly grasped the doorknob when it was pulled open from inside. She was in the kitchen before she could do more than blink and register the fact that she faced a very angry man.

"Where the hell have you been?" he demanded, his fingers biting into the flesh of her upper arms.

"Just out for a short walk. I saw Venita and talked to her, so I wasn't alone."

If possible, he looked angrier.

"There was no danger," she quickly added. "I, uh, got some information from her. She thinks something may happen here soon."

"Go on," Ty told her, hardly moving his lips.

"Yes, well, she says someone told her I

might be in danger and that if anything happened, I should stay inside. Ty, I know who the person was that warned her."

He ignored her information. A muscle moved in his throat. "I thought you were kidnapped or some damned thing. I was about to call in the FBI."

She squirmed under his hand. "You're hurting my arm."

He released his hold on her arm. His chest lifted in a deep breath, but he didn't say anything else. Wheeling around, he went to the phone and called Shane.

"He'll be over in a few minutes," Ty said, hanging up.

"Why? What's going on?"

Ty poured a cup of coffee and headed for the study without saying another word to her. She prepared her own cup and joined him. He was sitting on the sofa. She sat with him. He draped an arm around her shoulders and held her close.

The sheriff walked in unannounced twenty minutes later. He, too, poured a cup of coffee before coming to the study. "Let's hear it," he said.

Ty turned to her. "Tell him what Venita told you."

She repeated the entire episode, starting with the phone call.

"I'm glad you were cautious about going out to the stable. I wonder why she was afraid to talk on the phone."

"Bugged?" Carly suggested.

Ty unscrewed the covers on the receiver. "Nothing here," he reported. "I'll check all the ranch phones tomorrow."

"Do that," Shane advised. He studied Carly over the rim of his cup while he took a drink.

"What are you thinking?" Ty demanded.

She looked from one to the other as the men communicated without words.

"She might be the thing to draw Hodkin into the open if he's the one behind the thefts."

"No," Ty stated. He stood as if ready to fight, stance wide, hands formed into fists.

"How?" she asked. "I'd like to help."

"I got a report on him from Montana," Shane continued as if neither Ty nor she had spoken. "He was suspected of being in on a rash of extortions and robberies, but they had no conclusive proof. The problem stopped once he was out of the area, though.''

"Ha, he is a crook just as I thought." Carly flashed Ty a triumphant glance. She turned back to Shane. "But how can I draw him out?"

"He seems to have taken a dislike to you for some reason."

"She bashed him with a rock," Ty put in. "And she's not going to get involved. It's too dangerous."

"For you, too," she reminded him. "You slugged him. He's the type to carry a grudge to his grave."

"Then you can use me as the Judas goat, not her," Ty informed his brother.

She and the sheriff looked at him, then each other.

Shane shook his head. "Actually, I don't have a plan to use anyone. I was wondering if Hodkin plans to hit the ranch. Having Carly here could be an added attraction for him, a way of laughing in your face," he told Ty.

"I think you're right," she told Shane. "William must be his contact here. I think he's the one who told Venita to warn me off if there's trouble.''

''William?'' Shane questioned.

''The replacement for Hodkin. He's good with the horses. I was thinking of keeping him full-time. Carly's right. Venita works with William. He must have told her to stay out of the way, or she overheard him and suspected something, then decided to warn Carly.''

Shane stood. ''I'll do some checking and call you when I have news. By the way, Jonathan is getting restless. Tending a baby isn't as much fun as he thought it would be.''

''I'll follow you home and bring him back.''

''I thought I'd drop him off in the morning. He wants to give Carly another riding lesson. I think things will be quiet for the weekend.'' The sheriff headed for the door.

Ty walked with him.

Carly heard them murmuring in the kitchen for a minute before she heard the door open and close, then the smooth purr of the sheriff's utility vehicle driving off into the dark.

When Ty returned to the family room, she turned to him with a happy smile. ''This will make the local headlines. We'll be famous for breaking up the gang.'' She stood and flung herself into his arms, too elated to care about the scowl on his face.

He remained unyielding another moment, then his arms swept around her and he crushed her so close she could hardly breathe.

''When I returned and you were gone...'' He let the words sink into the silence of the house.

''I'm fine,'' she assured him, realizing his anger was a reflection of his concern for her. Her heart leapt around like a gazelle in the confines of her chest. Whether he admitted it or not, he cared for her.

She tilted her head back. ''Kiss me,'' she demanded, needing the security of his passion around her at that moment.

Emotion rippled through his eyes, too fast for her to read, then he lifted her and started toward the steps that led to the bedroom. ''I will,'' he promised huskily. ''I will.''

Carly spent a wonderful weekend with her two favorite men. The only danger she encountered was losing her seat on the horse she rode and her heart to the Macklin clan. Jonathan showed her how to twirl a lariat, then Ty taught them how to lasso a fence post. She and Jonathan practiced on a calf, but a moving target proved too difficult for them.

Laughing and teasing, they ate tortillas stuffed with chicken, cheese, beans and rice with Martha and Buck and the other couple, Mary and Chuck, in the ranch kitchen. William was off for the weekend. So was Venita.

On Sunday, Ty took her and Jonathan to an all-night restaurant at the interstate exchange. They ate hamburgers piled high with onion and mushrooms and melting cheese, spicy french fries that looked like curls, and finished with apple pie for dessert.

"What's your schedule this week?" Ty asked, resting his arms along the back of the booth across from her. Jonathan yawned and snuggled against him.

"I have merchandise to pick up Monday. The carpet will go in then, too. Other stuff will arrive Tuesday. On Wednesday, I'm going to wallpaper a chest to store sweaters in."

"Less than two weeks before the opening," he commented.

"Yes."

"Nervous?"

"Some." She met his eyes. "A lot," she admitted.

His sympathetic chuckle filled her with happiness. His gaze wandered over her, reminding her of the hours she'd spent in his arms during the night. He had touched her everywhere with his hands and his mouth before stretching his big, graceful body over hers for the final intimacy.

Warmth seeped through her. Being with him invoked a wonderful sense of well-being in her. In his arms, her world seemed right.

It came to her that the loneliness that had haunted her most of her life was gone. In its place were a man and his son, both so very dear to her.

Back at the house, a message waited from Shane. Hodkin had been in another brawl and was in jail. He didn't think there was any danger to her or Ty at the present.

"You can stay on here. If you want to," Ty said while the tape on the answering machine was rewinding.

"I was wondering if I was still invited."

She shot him a questioning glance. "Maybe I should go?"

He didn't return her smile, but simply gazed at her as if thinking of something far removed from them and the moment. "Not yet," he finally said.

To leave him and not see him every day was going to hurt. She swallowed against the knot that formed inside and tried to figure out how she had let this happen to her, how cool, levelheaded Carly Lightfoot, who wasn't going to depend on anyone for anything ever again, had fallen head over heels in love with a man who'd vowed the same.

Well, she reasoned, a person didn't let love happen. The heart did its own thing without orders from the brain. Maybe his was as insane as hers.

Carly wrapped up the decorating of her shop. She was ready to put the merchandise on display. She worked late Tuesday, Wednesday and Thursday, choosing to stay in the bed-and-breakfast inn those nights due to rain in the valley. It snowed on the mountains. Friday was the first sunshine they'd had all week.

She felt like kicking up her heels. Things were going as planned in her business. And she was invited to Ty's house for dinner. Jonathan had called and issued the invitation.

The boy admired her tremendously. She felt the same about him. He'd decided he was going to have his own business when he grew up and sell stuff just like her.

Ty had listened with a sardonic gleam in his eyes. "He was going to be a rodeo star for a whole week after the roping lesson," he'd reminded her.

"I'm sure he'll go through several careers by the time he's old enough to have one."

"What did you want to be besides a famous boutique owner?" Ty had asked when he walked her to her car on Monday.

"Well, my best friend and I decided we were going to be rich, famous, have husbands who adored us, raise perfect children and live next door to each other." She smiled. "We actually will live in adjoining apartments when one becomes vacant next month."

"So one plan came true, and you're on your way to the rich-and-famous part."

She wrinkled her nose as she walked to her

car. He'd been strangely distant last weekend, even when he'd held her. He seemed to have a lot on his mind, none of which he was sharing with her.

Well, he had his own life. She wouldn't pry.

At the inn, she changed to navy slacks and a white long-sleeved sweater that could be worn on or off the shoulders due to a drawstring in the neckline. After slipping into boots, she grabbed a warm parka and headed out again.

She did some shopping for toiletries, returned, then read until it was time to go to Ty's for the evening. He hadn't said anything about her staying the weekend. Her pride wouldn't let her ask. But she tucked an overnight bag in the trunk just in case.

At six, she went out to her car and drove the few miles from the inn to the ranch along the county road that ran nearly parallel to the interstate highway. It was a pleasant drive past ranches and orchards.

People here called anything over an acre a ranch, she'd learned. Thus, there were chicken ranches, cattle ranches and just plain ranches where the ranchers grew pears and pistachios instead of livestock.

For someone whose family had been there since pioneer days, Ty was remarkably free of conceit about it. He was a complicated person, but not arrogant. She liked that about him.

Her thoughts were interrupted by the sounds of sirens on the interstate. When she arrived at the Stop sign where the exit was, she watched two county sheriff's cars take the road she wanted. She followed them.

When they pulled into the Macklin driveway, fear squeezed the air from her lungs. She turned in and drove directly to Ty's house. A deputy sheriff stopped her when she would have gone in.

"Sorry, miss, but you can't go in."

"I'm expected."

He shook his head. "My orders are no one gets in."

"What's happened? Is Ty…is someone hurt?"

The young policeman hesitated, then leaned near her. "It's the boy. Someone snatched him—"

"Jonathan? Kidnapped?" She pressed a

hand to her heart as the horror of it hit her. "When? How?"

He shrugged. "We don't know. The bus let him off at the end of the drive after school. He started walking home according to the driver, but the kid disappeared before he got to the house."

"You've checked with the others on the ranch, with Martha and Mary? He's not at their houses?"

"No. Ty finished a call and walked down to meet his son as he usually does. He went all the way to the end of the road, but there was no sign of the boy."

"I've got to see Ty."

"Sorry, I can't—"

"You don't understand. Jonathan invited me to dinner tonight. He was going to cook. I'm going in."

She gave the young officer a stern frown and sailed past him to the kitchen door. She walked in without knocking.

Shane was on the phone. Tina was sitting in a kitchen chair nursing the baby. Ty stood with his hands gripping the back of another chair. He could have been a statue, he stood so still.

"Ty," she murmured, her heart bleeding for him. She ignored Shane's warning glance and went to Ty.

He didn't move.

She paused, uncertain what to do. Lifting a trembling hand, she touched his arm, wanting desperately to comfort him. "Have you heard anything?" she asked softly.

He looked at her then, and she was struck by the fury in the ravaged gaze he turned on her.

"What are you doing here?" he demanded. "I told the cops not to let anybody in."

She dropped her hand from him and stepped back. "I told the man outside I was expected." Her words sounded flimsy, an excuse to barge in on a family that was suffering.

"There's enough trouble here without adding more."

Puzzled, she glanced at Tina, then Shane. Neither of them offered any insight into Ty's strange behavior.

"I didn't know about Jonathan until I got here," she said. "There wasn't anything on the radio about it."

"We're keeping it quiet until we get more

details from the kidnappers on what they want,'' Shane told her.

"Oh, yes. I see.''

She clamped her teeth into her bottom lip to stop its trembling. Ty looked as if he hated everybody, including her. A sickening thought occurred to her. Had Jonathan been taken because of her? Was Hodkin getting revenge on Ty for interfering in his vendetta on her when she clobbered him with a rock?

"Ty,'' she whispered, "Jonathan is smart. He'll be okay.''

His knuckles turned white as he gripped the chair. "A six-year-old? What can he do against someone like Hodkin?'' He turned to the deputy who'd followed her into the house. "Get her out of here. We don't have time for guests.''

The man looked at Shane, who nodded, then at Carly. She stared at Ty, unable to believe this was the man who had held her and kissed her a thousand times last Sunday night. Gathering what dignity she could, she walked out.

"Carly, wait.''

She faced Tina, who followed her across the lawn to her car. She trembled uncontrollably, knowing she shouldn't have barged in. She loved Ty and Jonathan, but she was the outsider here....

"He's hurting," Tina said gently, patting the baby's back so it would burp. "He doesn't mean it."

"He blames me," Carly choked out.

"He's lashing out at anyone who comes close. Don't let it hurt you. He knows, in his heart, that it isn't your fault. No one can predict what an evil person will do. Hodkin posted bail and was released. He took Jonathan hostage, and wants a plane to take him to Mexico. He says he'll turn Jonathan loose after he's out of the country."

"Oh, God." Carly closed her eyes.

"Shane and Ty are going to track them," Tina explained the plan to her. "Hodkin is holed up somewhere in the mountains. He called from a cellular phone, that much we know."

"What can I do?" Carly asked anxiously, wanting so badly to help. "It will kill Ty if something happens to Jonathan."

"He needs you, but he can't admit it. Stay. If things go wrong..." Tina swallowed hard.

"If things go wrong, he'll need you very, very much. Stay close."

"When are he and Shane leaving? I'll go with them—"

"Stay with me. We'll wait together. It will be a long night, I'm afraid." She looked toward the house. "They're going now, I think. Wait here."

Tina handed Carly the baby and hurried toward her husband and brother-in-law. The child started to fret. Carly automatically patted his back and swung her body to and fro to rock it.

Shane kissed his wife goodbye. He accepted a backpack from a deputy. Carly noted a rifle strapped to the pack. Ty had one on his, too. So did six other deputies.

They were going on a manhunt.

She suppressed a desperate need to go to Ty and touch him, however briefly, before he left. He didn't glance her way.

When the men left after listening intently to instructions from the sheriff, Tina came back to her. "Let's wait inside." She led the way into Ty's house. No one tried to stop Carly.

Tina put the sleeping baby in a carrier and

removed a roast from the oven. "Let's have dinner."

"I'm not hungry." Carly stood by the window.

"It doesn't do any good to starve. You'll only make yourself less effective." She dished up two plates and set the table. She took her place. "You're right. Jonathan is a smart kid. He won't do anything foolish. It wouldn't surprise me if he got away and came home on his own."

Carly nodded, but her confidence had faded. She strained to see the men, but they had disappeared into the woods, following a logging road. She studied the sky.

The sun was setting. Soon the light would fade and the darkness descend. If Jonathan did get away, what might happen to a child in the woods at night? She couldn't bear to think on it. Turning, she went to the table.

With an effort, she managed to get some of the food down. Ty had prepared an assortment of vegetables with the roast, and she ate a bite of each before putting the fork aside. This was to have been their supper, she realized.

"He's incredibly special," she murmured as

if realizing it that very moment. "How could any woman give up a man who can cook a pot roast?" She tried to smile at Tina, but her mouth wouldn't hold the pose. Her lips wobbled precariously before she pressed her napkin to them.

"Ty's learned a lot about himself the past couple of years," Tina replied. "He's learned to be a father. I think that's what saved him—his love for Jonathan."

"He used to drink quite a bit, I understand."

"Yes. That was during the final year of his marriage. Things were pretty rocky with him then, but he came through." She smiled wisely. "People do, you know. We live through some awful times, but we make it. Jonathan will, too. And so will you and Ty."

Carly shook her head. "He hates me, and he has a right. I did come here under false pretenses, thinking a ranch would be the perfect hideaway, as if the people were put here for my amusement. I interfered even though Elena told me to stay out of it."

"But what if you hadn't? What would have happened to Venita if you'd ignored her problems?"

"Does Shane know it's Hodkin who has Jonathan?"

"Yes. He's the one who called and demanded safe passage to Mexico. Two others have been arrested."

"Was William one of them?"

"I don't know anyone by that name."

Carly shook her head sorrowfully. "Venita is in love with him, I think. He told her to warn me. Ty protected me, thinking I was at risk. We never thought they'd take Jonathan."

Tina sighed and looked at the clock. "Why do the hours creep by when you want them to fly and fly when you want them to crawl?"

Carly woke to a shout from the backyard. She leapt from the sofa in the study and ran to the kitchen. Men were everywhere in the yard. More patrol cars arrived while she watched. She couldn't tell what was going on.

Then she saw Ty...and Jonathan.

He held his son in a tight embrace while the other deputies clapped him and Shane on the back and shoulders. She realized they were grinning. While she watched, Shane pushed

Hodkin, whose hands were handcuffed behind him, toward a squad car.

The young officer who'd stopped her earlier that evening got in the driver's side. Another deputy climbed in. With lights flashing, they turned and headed out toward the road. Taking the culprit to jail, she assumed.

Tina came over to stand beside her. "Thank God," she whispered. She smiled. "I knew Shane would get him back." She dashed out the door, going first to Jonathan and Ty. After giving them both a kiss, she went to her husband. Shane opened his arms and drew her inside. They kissed, briefly but passionately.

Carly became aware of the ache of tears in her throat. She waited nervously for Ty to come in the house.

After a few minutes, Shane spoke to his brother, then came into the house for the baby. He paused for a minute. "It went off without a hitch," he told Carly. "We found them at the cabin where Ty thought Hodkin would hole up. When he stepped outside, leaving Jonathan in the cabin, we simply surrounded him. He had no weapon, so it wasn't even a standoff." He grinned and headed out.

She watched as the other cars left. The sheriff took his family home in his patrol car. Jonathan and Ty came into the house.

"Carly," Jonathan said, his eyes alight with excitement, "I was kidnapped. Daddy and Uncle Shane rescued me."

"Yes, I see they did," she said unsteadily. Now that the danger was over, her control was slipping badly. She held her breath and waited for Ty to say something.

"I wasn't scared...well, not much. I was going to run away when he went to sleep."

The tears surged to her eyes. She blinked them back with an effort. "You're smart," she said, "like your father and uncle."

"Yeah," he agreed. "It was neat. But I'm glad to be home." He smiled at his father, then yawned hugely.

During the conversation, Ty hadn't glanced her way. When she stepped forward, wanting to go to him, he stopped her with a frown. "Jonathan needs to get to bed. He's had enough excitement." He paused. "Sorry about dinner."

"That's okay."

With blurred vision, she found her purse and

went to her car. During the drive back to the inn, the tears insisted on forming. She overcame them by willpower. Tears never solved a thing. They hadn't brought her parents back. They hadn't made her relatives want her. They certainly wouldn't dissolve the wall of distrust between her and Ty Macklin.

Chapter Thirteen

"Brody, I'm fine. Really," Carly spoke into the telephone to her foster brother. She tried to inject a mixture of firmness and lightness into her voice to dispel his concern for her.

"I don't think so," he stated in his usual manner, forming his own opinion no matter what she said.

The hum of electronic static came through the line as they both fell silent. "Well, I am," she insisted. "Listen, I've got to run out to the store. Opening day is this Friday. I'll talk to you later."

There was another brief silence. "Why don't you visit the ranch for a while?"

"Are you there?" she asked.

"For now. I'll be heading for New York in a couple of days."

"Doing what?"

"Checking out some things for a client."

"Is it dangerous?" She couldn't keep the worry out of her voice. Brody could be reckless at times, and a private investigator could get into sticky situations.

"No, merely boring...but rewarding." He laughed softly.

"What are you going to do with all your money?" she teased, half-seriously. "You can't take it with you."

"I'm working on that."

She smiled. Brody was determined to have enough money to be independent of anyone and anything. She wondered what would happen to his fierce need for freedom when he fell in love.

"Yeah, right. Good luck. I've got to go. I still have a million things to do before Friday." She paused, wishing he were there so they could really talk. "Come see me when you get a chance, okay?"

"I will."

"Promise?"

"Yes."

After they said goodbye, she sat by the phone and felt the loneliness of her life crash in on her. Gritting her teeth, she dressed and headed for the shop to rearrange it for the seventh time in two days.

On the car radio, the big story of the week was winding down. To everyone's surprise, William turned out to be an undercover FBI agent who was also investigating Hodkin. It seemed the petty thief was low man in an international ring. They stole farm equipment, took it to Mexico, where the equipment was stripped for parts that were then sold to eastern markets.

Shane and Ty were the local heroes because of the rescue of Jonathan and the capture of Hodkin, who'd been left behind by his other two companions in crime when they made their getaway. William had picked them up before they crossed the state line.

For the first time in her life, Carly found herself the object of national interest when her part in Hodkin's revenge became known. He'd come to the ranch to force her to drive him on his escape route, but had seen Jonathan and decided on a better plan.

After giving an exclusive interview to the local station on her contretemps with the desperado, she'd been bombarded with questions when other news services jumped on the story of her defense of Venita and Ty's defense of her.

For two days, the kidnapping had been the prime-time story, then the wreck of a cattle truck on the interstate highway had superseded it. Such was life.

She'd seen Ty once during the weekend. They had been at the TV station at the same time. He was leaving as she was arriving. He'd spoken to her as if they were casual acquaintances and had introduced her to his ex-wife.

His former wife had flown in to see that her son hadn't suffered a trauma from the ordeal. She was a beautiful woman.

Carly had watched her being interviewed on television, seated between Ty and Jonathan. They looked like a model family—father, mother and son.

She pushed the hurtful thought aside. She had places to go and people to see, she reminded herself, passing a truck on the winding road to the resort. But she kept remembering those few wonderful days she'd spent at his house.

Men burn and women yearn....

He'd cooled off fast enough when his former wife had appeared. The woman was staying at the ranch. Naturally.

Carly bit back the thought. She sounded like a jealous shrew and she had no right, none at all. That was the thing to remember in an affair. Neither person had any rights over the other.

She summoned anger to keep other emotions at bay while she parked and went inside the resort lodge.

A new box of jewelry had arrived. She opened it and sorted through the items. Elena and her daughters had done a lovely job, using the colors Carly had suggested to go with the sweaters she'd purchased. There were earrings and bracelets to match, too. She arranged the new items in artfully casual displays with necklaces trailing out of dresser drawers amid an array of colorful scarves.

Hours later, she stepped back and admired

the display of goods in the tiny store. Perfect. She couldn't think of another thing to do. The owner of the resort had planned a media event for the grand opening tomorrow, including a spot on the midday news. She had to find something to wear.

Going to her car, she contemplated the evening ahead. After shopping for an outfit, she had nothing to do but go home.

Alys would be disappointed in her. The young woman thought the life of an entrepreneur must be exciting and glamorous.

Carly smiled, feeling the irony all the way to her soul. Well, she'd learned not to expect too much of life....

"Miss Lightfoot?"

She whirled around. She was getting darned careless when a man could approach within five feet without her noticing.

"Yes?"

"I've been trying to get in touch with you, but no one would tell me your number."

"It's unlisted."

He nodded. "I'm Samuel Jumpers. My family owns several department stores...."

*   *   *

"How much did you say?" Carly was incredulous.

He named a salary that would have knocked her off her feet had she been standing. Fortunately, she was seated in a comfortable booth at the Rogue Mountain Resort while the corporate mogul tried to talk her into taking a position in marketing.

The Jumpers family owned three large department-store chains, each catering to a different clientele. Sam told her they were aiming for number one in the Western retail market in each chain, and she was part of that effort.

She shook her head. The offer was three times what she'd ever made before.

"Don't decide now," Sam cautioned, taking her negative shake to mean she was saying no. "Think about it."

She was so stunned she couldn't have thought her way out of a paper bag at the moment. Her mind boggled as she thought of the money she would make.

There was only one catch. The family headquarters was in St. Louis. They wanted her to work out of the home office.

So they could keep an eye on her?

Probably. However, she'd have free rein to set the shops up, hire managers and choose their suppliers and merchandise.

It was too much. She needed to share the news, to mull over the possibilities with someone before making a decision. She'd call…who would she call? Isa was at the theater, doing the play. Brody was busy….

"St. Louis isn't high on my list of priorities," she told Mr. Jumpers. "I don't like cities."

"Would another fifty thousand sweeten the deal?" he asked.

Carly shook her head in disbelief again. The family must be desperate if they were willing to pay that kind of money for an unknown to come in to advise them.

"I know this isn't your first offer," he continued when she said nothing. "You got prime-time national coverage last week, and your success in Chicago was pointed out to me by my banker. He mentioned you were sure to be in high demand."

"You seem to know a lot," she murmured, concealing surprise. She'd had a call from the head of a group of venture capitalists who wanted to start a chain of vacation boutiques patterned after The Cricket Cage. She was supposed to be thinking over their offer, too.

"It's my business," he reminded her, his smile confident.

"Mr. Jumpers—"

"'Sam,'" he corrected.

She realized the look in his eyes was one of interest, male to female interest. It startled her.

"Sam. I'm grateful—and I admit I'm tempted—but I think I'm going to pass on your generous offer."

He shook his head. "I refuse to accept that. You haven't thought about the advantages. You'd have money available to develop your ideas on a grand scale, as well as a showcase for your talents. The opportunity to explore new terrain—"

His persuasive words were interrupted by the arrival of several people at the table next to them. Her throat closed when she saw who it was, and for a second, she couldn't breathe.

Ty Macklin, his sister-in-law, Tina, and his ex-wife were among the group. Ty sat at the end of the table...no more than three feet from her. He hadn't seen her yet. She gazed out the window as if spellbound by the view of the mountains, thus keeping her back to the room.

When the newcomers were seated, Sam Jumpers renewed his argument. "It's a good time to move. Houses are at their lowest in years. The interest rates are good, too."

Carly shifted nervously, not liking the thought that Ty could overhear every word they said. "I'll think about it," she promised, and tried to turn the conversation. "I hope our meal arrives soon. I was so busy today I forgot to eat lunch."

"St. Louis has some of the finest restaurants in the world," Sam assured her. He gave her a sly grin. "I'll personally take you out on the town your first night there."

She flicked an uneasy glance over her shoulder...and met Ty Macklin's surprised, then furious, gaze. Oh, well, it was only a matter of time before they'd run into each other. Better to face it now and get it over. She gave him a brilliant smile. "Ty. How nice to see you. You too, Tina."

Her tone was just right—neutral, friendly but not gushing, conversational without being either cool or warm.

His eyes flicked from her to her companion and back. With a lowering of his dark eyebrows, he nodded to her, then to Sam.

Tina wasn't so restrained. ''Carly,'' she said warmly, rising and coming to her. She bent and gave Carly a hug. ''Who's this?'' she demanded. ''A new man in town, and you're keeping him to yourself?'' Tina waited with an expectant smile on her face.

Carly groaned silently, then introduced them. ''Tina Macklin, Sam Jumpers,'' she said, refusing to explain who the man was.

''Hello. Are you from around here?'' Tina asked, not at all put off by Carly's attitude.

''No, St. Louis,'' he replied, ''but I wish I were. Beautiful women must grow on trees.''

''Of course,'' Tina said with a laugh. ''Have I seen you before? You look familiar.''

He told her the name of the company. Carly hoped Tina would let it go at that.

No such luck.

''Oh, of course. Your family owns more square footage of department-store space than any other chain in the States.'' She glanced at Carly, then turned back to Sam. ''Are you trying to steal Carly away from us?''

"I've made her an offer," he admitted. "A very good one."

Tina made the connection at once. "Your headquarters is in St. Louis, isn't it?"

"Yes," he said. They both looked at Carly.

So did Ty, she noticed. No expression showed on his handsome face, though. She could have been a stranger.

"What a wonderful chance for you," Tina said sincerely.

"Say that again," Sam requested. "She doesn't seem to realize it."

Tina's eyebrows rose. "You've refused?"

"No, I'm thinking it over," Carly stated firmly, feeling that things—her life, her future—were slipping out of her hands. She wanted to be in complete control when she decided her fate.

"Perhaps she's holding out for a better offer," Ty suggested.

"I've already had a better offer," she informed him. "From ABC Capitalists," she added when he looked skeptical.

Tina gasped while Sam Jumpers looked disappointed. "I can see I'm wasting my time," he said. "You should have told me."

"I turned them down, too." Carly gave Ty a chilly smile. "As I said before, I don't much care for big cities." She turned back to Samuel Jumpers. "But perhaps I could learn to like St. Louis."

He relaxed and beamed at her. "I'll do everything I can to ensure that." His eyes sent out signals of approval and awareness of her as a woman.

Ty gave a snort. She lifted her chin. It felt nice to be appreciated, to be looked upon as an attractive woman without a wall of anger hitting her in the face.

She'd hardly gotten settled, but maybe it was time for her to move on. She swallowed against the depression that threatened to overpower her, refusing to give in to such weakness.

When their food arrived, she was relieved. Tina returned to her seat after she'd extracted a promise from Carly to come for a small cocktail party the following night.

During the meal, Sam droned on and on about St. Louis and its many advantages for her. He painted a glowing scenario of her future success. She wished he'd shut up and eat so they could leave. With every bite, she was aware of Ty and his disapproving countenance, which she saw every time she glanced that way.

When dinner was finally over, down to the last cup of coffee, they rose and departed. She said goodbye to Sam in the parking lot and got in her own car to drive home. She took his card and promised to call within a week.

Driving to the inn, she saw her life unroll before her like the highway, a vast grayness stretching toward the horizon with no end in sight. Once inside, she roamed the spacious room in restless anger.

She wished she'd never met Ty Macklin. He only reminded her of all the things that were absent from her life, things she hadn't missed until she'd opened her heart to him.

On Saturday morning, she separated her clothes into piles and took some to the cleaners, others to the laundry. Returning, she put the clean clothes away and sighed heavily, then jerked when the doorbell rang three times before she could get to it.

Her heart knocked against her ribs at the impatient summons. She flew across the room and opened the door.

''Brody,'' she said stupidly.

He gave her a thorough appraisal, then grunted as if satisfied that she really was all right. ''I thought I'd drop by,'' he said in his usual gruff manner, and walked in.

She closed the door and gave him a sardonic smile. ''You're supposed to be in New York. A far drop, isn't it?''

His broad shoulders moved in a shrug as he paced like a black panther to the sliding glass doors that led out to a patio. He was a tall, lean man with black hair and a dark, piercing gaze. He rarely laughed, but when he did, it changed his rough features in a manner that startled those who saw it for the first time.

Not that he became handsome. He'd lived a hard life, and it showed in a nose that had been broken twice. A scar puckered his right temple where a bullet had skimmed the flesh, giving his face a rakish air and the observer the impression that here was a man who didn't flinch in the face of danger.

Carly smiled as a rush of affection came over her. Brody wasn't handsome, but when he smiled, his teeth were a dazzling white in his swarthy face. Like her, he tanned easily and could pass for Hispanic or Native American, if he wished.

"Coffee?" she offered, then remembered he was always hungry. "I think I have a tin of cookies somewhere."

"Fine." He followed her to the side table where she kept a coffee maker and watched while she prepared the snack.

"I could go out for sandwiches," she volunteered.

He shook his head. "I had lunch on the plane. It was enough. I came to see how you were."

She wrinkled her nose at him. "You were always a worrywart."

"You always kept everything to yourself," he snapped right back. "You've lost weight."

"A little."

"He's not worth it."

Her head jerked around as if pulled by a string. "What makes you think there's a man involved?"

"Your eyes are sad." His smile was mocking.

She sighed. "You see right through me."

"So tell me about it."

For the next two hours, she did. When the telephone rang and she heard Tina's voice, Carly felt a wave of relief when she realized Brody gave her a perfect excuse to get out of the party.

"Come have early dinner with us at six," Tina said.

"Oh, I meant to call and tell you I won't be there at all. I have a guest from out of town."

"Bring him."

"Uh, he isn't much for parties," Carly explained.

"I'll go," Brody spoke right behind her.

Tina heard him. "Good. We'll expect you both at six." She said goodbye and hung up.

Carly replaced the receiver and gave Brody a scowl. "Why did you do that? It'll only cause trouble."

"Good," he said.

She sighed as a sense of foreboding broke over her. It was going to be a difficult night.

Brody changed from his jeans to a suit before they left for the dinner at Tina's house.

"Nice digs" was his comment on the Macklin home when she pulled into the driveway.

She stopped by the sidewalk to the Victorian mansion. There were no other cars in the drive. A nervous tremor raced over her.

Brody looked the place over as they walked toward the front door. His normally wary manner went with his profession of private investigator. A surge of affection for him made her smile. He was here to check out the cause of her unhappiness.

She hooked her hand through his arm and gave it a squeeze. "Are you going to sock Ty Macklin?" she asked.

"Do you want me to?" He cocked one black eyebrow at her.

Laughing, she shook her head, then reached up to kiss his cheek in gratitude for his concern. That was the way Ty discovered them when he appeared from around the corner of the house and bounded up on the broad front porch.

He took in the scene without comment, but his eyes, when he looked at her, were filled with some emotion she couldn't read. A tremor shook her when he came forward with a solemn smile.

"Hello, come on in. Tina is expecting us," he said. "I'm Ty Macklin," he introduced himself to Brody.

"Brody Smith."

The men shook hands, then Ty opened the door, and they were engulfed in the domesticity of the older Macklin brother's home.

Shane met them in the foyer, the new baby in his arms. Jonathan was with him. "Hi," the boy sang out. "Guess what, Carly? I've been helping with the baby. He likes me."

"Of course he does," she agreed. "He's lucky to have a cousin like you to teach him all about things."

"Who's this?" Jonathan asked, looking Brody over.

She introduced Brody to Shane and Jonathan, then Tina when she came bustling out of the kitchen. "Mrs. Perkins has everything under control," she told them. "Let's go into the living room and chat. Where are you from, Brody?"

"Portland."

"Oh, my mom and stepfather live there."

She led the way into the living room. Shane and Jonathan put the baby to bed upstairs and rejoined them in a few minutes.

Picture of domestic bliss, Carly thought wryly, trying not to let her glance stray to Ty too often. Brody had no such qualms. His dark gaze fastened on Ty each time Ty spoke. She realized Brody was drawing Ty out, asking all kinds of questions about his plans for the ranch and his life in general, but doing it subtly, slipping in his queries in a natural manner.

As the evening progressed, she became increasingly anxious to get away. Each time she looked at Ty, he seemed to be watching her. When she licked her lips, she saw his eyes take in the action. It made her nervous.

After dinner, they returned to the living room for coffee. Just as she was beginning to breathe easier, Tina left and returned with the baby. ''Would you hold him for a minute?'' she asked.

Before Carly could respond, Ian was placed in her arms. She stared down into his tiny face and felt herself melt inside. She hadn't held him since the night of Jonathan's rescue.

''He's grown,'' she murmured.

"I'll get the coffee," Tina said, and left.

Shane and Brody were talking about guns. They went to the study to look over a collection of antique rifles. That left Ty and Jonathan with her and the baby. Jonathan came over to the sofa and pressed in close beside her.

"He doesn't look like much now," Jonathan explained, "but he'll be different when he grows some."

Ty came over and sat on the other side of her. "But babies are still pretty cute, even if they do have big heads." He and Jonathan laughed.

She made an incoherent murmur. Her throat wouldn't open enough for her to speak. Heat seemed to sear her body. She realized Ty was also pressed against her as he leaned over to admire the baby.

"Do you like babies?" he asked softly.

She looked at him. A mistake, for their lips were no more than four inches apart. His eyes seemed to bore into hers. She was held immobile by that probing gaze.

"Dad and I do," Jonathan piped up. "Don't we, Dad?"

"Yes." His eyes never left hers.

Carly swallowed and looked back at the baby, who opened his eyes and peered at the three faces bending over him. He smiled.

"Look, he likes you, too, Carly," Jonathan said. He waved a rattle to attract the baby's attention, then made comical faces to amuse his cousin.

"It's probably a gas bubble. I've heard that's what makes babies appear to smile during the first weeks."

"No," Ty said. "I think Jonathan is right. He likes you."

His breath played lightly over her temple and cheek, fanning a few loose strands of hair so that they tickled. She brushed her cheek against her shoulder to stop the feeling and touched him by accident. She straightened at once, so acutely aware of his strong masculine presence, it was almost a pain.

He smoothed the strands back for her. "Are you going to St. Louis?" he asked in a low voice.

"I don't know. It's a good offer...but I haven't decided." She couldn't think when he was so near. Her blood seemed to thicken, and her heart pounded furiously.

"You didn't like the venture capitalists?"

That brought her gaze back to his. "How did you know about that?" she demanded, taking refuge in annoyance. It was amazing how fast news traveled in small towns.

"I listened to your conversation." He smiled briefly, then perused her with a solemn expression. "You'd never be happy in Chicago. You weren't before."

"How do you know?" She cast him a defiant glance, then smiled when she realized Jonathan and the baby were both looking at her.

Ty heaved a sigh as if exasperated with her. "How long is Smith staying?"

"I'm not sure," she hedged. "He's supposed to be in New York tomorrow, so I guess he'll leave in the morning." She bounced Ian up and down when he puckered up. "There, there. Don't cry. Mommy will be back soon." She hoped.

Jonathan waved the rattle in front of Ian's face, but that didn't distract him. He began to wail. She wondered what to do.

"Here. I'll take him up and change him."

Ty slipped his hands under hers and scooped the child into his arms.

Carly watched him leave the room, Jonathan right beside him, giving advice and offering to help.

"I'd appreciate that, son," he told the boy.

Ty handled children with the same easy grace he displayed while working on the ranch. Nothing fazed him. He was a wonderful father to his son and would be a wonderful uncle to Shane's son, as Shane was with Jonathan. The Macklins were a tight-knit, loving family for children to grow up in. It would be such a pleasure to be part of it....

She went to the window and stared out at the night sky until she could once again control the pain that raged through her. She couldn't afford to let herself think along those lines.

Ty didn't trust her. He thought women used men for their own advantage. And of course she *had,* in a way, when she'd first come to the ranch...to find herself. She hadn't expected to find a father and son who'd steal her heart. She wondered where the ex-wife was. Maybe she'd be there later.

Carly decided to give the St. Louis job some definite thought.

Tina came in with a coffee tray. "It looks like the men have deserted us," she commented, placing the tray on the coffee table.

"Ty and Jonathan went to change the baby. I think Shane and Brody are still discussing guns." She returned to the sofa. "When are your other guests due?"

Tina looked a little embarrassed. "That was a ploy to get you here. I was afraid you wouldn't come if you thought it was only a family dinner."

"What happened to Jonathan's mother?"

"She returned to New York when the kidnapping wasn't the big story anymore." Tina wrinkled her nose. "Sorry, I didn't mean to sound so cynical."

The men ambled back into the room before Carly could think of a reply. She forced down a cup of coffee, then rose and said it was time to go.

Brody looked rather surprised at her abrupt announcement. He and Shane were talking about the latest investigative techniques as if they were long-lost buddies. He looked at his watch. "You're right. My plane leaves at seven in the morning. I'll have to drag her out of bed to get me to the airport on time."

Carly felt a flush warm her face and quickly looked at Ty. He smiled and gave her a sexy once-over. She knew he was thinking of the times they'd been in bed. Memories of his hands sweeping over her in endless caresses brought the blood to her cheeks.

She rushed Brody with his thanks and farewells to their hosts. In the car, she breathed a sigh of relief at getting through the evening without catastrophe. Brody had been known to hit first and ask questions later, but he'd been perfectly at ease with the Macklin brothers.

"Good men, Shane and Ty," he murmured, reading her thoughts. "You could do worse."

She gave him an exasperated glare. "What's that supposed to mean? I'm not doing anything with either of them."

"Well, not with Shane, naturally. He's married. But Ty is okay. He'll make you a good husband."

"I'm not…there's nothing…I explained all that earlier," she finally declared, amazed by his obtuseness.

"Oh, there's something," he contradicted. "Be cool and don't make any commitments to St. Louis right away."

She tried arguing with him, but Brody could be as tight-mouthed as a miser with solid-gold teeth when he chose. She gave up shortly before they reached her place with its bedroom and tiny sitting room.

Once inside, she flipped on a lamp. "I'll make up the sofa. You can have my bed."

"I don't mind bunking out here."

"No, you're too tall. Your feet would dangle over the sofa arm." She headed for the bedroom to fetch the sheets and a blanket. "Let me get into my pajamas and brush my teeth, then you can have it."

She went into the bedroom, changed clothes, washed up and was back in ten minutes.

"Pretty good," Brody complimented. "You're still the fastest female in the bathroom that I've ever known."

Carly made up the sofa into a bed. She dropped the blanket at the end of the sofa in case she needed it later. Taking a seat, she asked, "How many females have you known well enough to time their bathing routines?"

He shot her one of his don't-meddle-in-my-private-life looks, but she didn't flinch. He shared several characteristics with Ty, stubbornness being one of them. "Not many," he said.

"Have you ever been in love?"

"No." He grinned and tousled her bangs on his way to the bedroom. "And I don't intend to."

"Sometimes it sneaks up on a person."

"Not me. I keep moving so it doesn't." He gave her an arrogant smile and went into the bedroom.

Carly hugged a pillow to her chest and thought of her own overconfident plans. First, she was going to be a big success in her career, then she was going to find the perfect man, who wouldn't interfere in her life in any way, marry and have two perfect children.

So here she was, thirty years old, in love with a man who wanted her and hated her because of it, with no mention of marriage or children in sight.

But she had achieved her goal in her career. She was where she wanted to be, and that satisfied her. Sort of. Except it would be hard to stay in the area and run into Ty, which was inevitable. Moving to St. Louis was looking more and more interesting.

She sighed. At the same instant, the doorbell rang.

Every cell in her body clenched. The doorbell rang again…then again…an impatient call for attention.

She went to see who was calling. It was too early for Isa to be free from the theater, she thought with a frown. Unless it was an emergency.

She peered through the peephole and gasped. With nerveless fingers, she opened the door.

"May I come in?" Ty requested formally. When she moved, he stepped inside and halted at the edge of the marble tiles covering the foyer, his eyes riveted on the sofa bed. "Is this a private party, or can anybody join?" he asked in a husky voice.

"Private," she informed him.

The bedroom door opened. Brody looked at Ty, then her. She felt heat flood her cheeks.

"I wondered when you were going to show up," Brody said.

Ty nodded. "I was going to wait until you left, but..." He shrugged as if that explained everything.

Apparently it did. Brody grinned. "Good luck."

Carly wondered if they had both gone crazy. "And it isn't even a full moon," she muttered.

Ty shifted so he could watch her, which he proceeded to do with an intensity that left her shaken.

"I think I'll go for a walk," Brody said.

She realized he still had on his jacket. "It's nearly eleven o'clock," she reminded him. She remembered she had on her pajamas.

"A short walk." He flicked a meaningful glance at Ty and walked out the door.

A nervous trill ran along Carly's nerves. Ty faced her with his hands in his pockets, a frown on his face.

"I meant to wait until tomorrow, after Brody left, for this, but I couldn't," he said.

She tried to make some sense of the statement. She pushed a strand of hair off her temple. "I'd really like to go to bed. It's late. I'm tired."

"I have something to say. It will only take a minute."

She hesitated, then nodded, resigned to listening to whatever he had to confess.

"I apologize for the way I've treated you since…these past few days. The attraction between us, then the kidnapping, the press…it was overwhelming."

Amazement widened her eyes. "A Macklin, apologizing? What is the world coming to?"

"Don't get smart," he ordered, giving her a stern frown. He crossed the narrow area between them and stood in front of her. He reached out, then drew back without touching her.

"That night when Jonathan was taken, I wasn't thinking straight. I know you care for him and wouldn't do anything that would put him in jeopardy. It wasn't your fault, but I blamed you anyway. It seemed every time I allowed a woman into my life, bad things happened. Will you forgive me?" he asked so sincerely she was taken aback. The sardonic smile she'd summoned slipped from her lips.

"Of course. There's nothing to forgive. I shouldn't have rushed in. I had no business

being there. It was just…I was worried. Jonathan is such a sweetheart. And I felt so terribly guilty. Hodkin was getting back at you
because of me.''

The tension built. Being alone with him, her
emotions running high after his unexpected
apology, she knew she was too vulnerable to
his presence. She turned her back to him and
gripped her hands together as longing perme-
ated her being.

She heard him move, then she felt the
strangest sensation on her neck…a soft, fleet-
ing sensation like the brush of a feather or a
butterfly's wing.

''Oh,'' she gasped.

He kissed her again. ''I've wanted to do that
for a long time,'' he murmured, laying his
cheek against the side of her head. His hands
clasped her shoulders while he trailed kisses
along her temple. ''So many things I'd missed
until you came along.''

''What are you doing?'' she managed to
whisper.

''Making love to you.'' He turned her to
face him. ''If you'll let me.''

She couldn't think what to say. Surely she

hadn't heard him right. "I... Why do you want to?"

The corners of his mouth curved upward into an entrancing smile. "Why wouldn't I? I'm a man, and you're a beautiful woman."

"I'm not."

"Are we going to argue about it?" He cupped her face between his hands. "You're beautiful to me. Don't you know that?" His voice dropped to a husky murmur, gritty and somewhat desperate in tone. "Don't you know how much I love you?"

She shook her head and grasped his arms to stop the world from spinning like mad.

"I do." He gave her a little shake, then ran his thumbs under her chin and stroked the sensitive flesh there. "I didn't want to, but I couldn't stop. It made me angry. You were irresistible, and I went down for the count. That can scare a man, you know."

He brushed his lips across hers. All the barriers she'd erected during the past week crumbled and disappeared. "It scared me, too," she confessed.

"Mm-hmm," he crooned sympathetically.

He kissed her nose and her eyes, her cheeks and her ears.

Her heart careened all around her chest before settling down to a bone-rattling beat. She raised her mouth to his, wanting his kiss on her lips. The need to respond, to show him how much she cared, washed over her.

When he continued moving his lips over her face, she made an impatient sound and caught his tawny hair in her hands, forcing him to be still. Then she kissed him, planting her lips and her body firmly against his, loving the feel of him against her.

"How soon do you think your brother will return?" he said against her mouth at one point.

She gave a muffled reply. His hands slipped under her pajama top. He explored the bare skin of her back, then her sides, and finally sought her breasts. Wildfire leapt through her. She pushed him backward.

He fell on the sofa with a grunt of surprise. She followed, lying over him and trying to unfasten his shirt at the same time.

"Don't be so aggressive," he scolded, laughing at the soft, impatient exclamations she made. He caught her hands and pressed them over his head, bringing her against his chest. "God, I love you. Do that some more."

"What?" she whispered, biting his earlobe.

"Everything."

He crushed her to him and ravaged her with his kisses until she squirmed helplessly against him. She got his shirt open and her hands on his body. She caressed him wildly, feeling the passion build to unbearable heights.

"Ty," she murmured over and over.

"What, darling? Tell me what you want."

"I want you to touch me." She was desperate for it.

He cupped her breasts while they kissed again. She rubbed the hard crest in his jeans. He pulled away and held her hands.

"If I stay here, we'll make love. Brody will be back soon."

She looked at him in disappointment. "I forgot about him. It's just that, when you kiss me, I want you so. Ty, did you mean it? You really love me? It isn't just passion?"

He took a deep breath. "I love you with all my heart. With all my passion, too." He didn't ask, but his eyes questioned her. She knew he needed the words, too.

"Oh, yes," she whispered. "I love you... love you...love you." With each pause, she kissed him hungrily.

He laughed and scooped her up against him. "Behave. Or I won't be responsible for the consequences. We need to talk."

When Brody returned, they were sitting circumspectly at the dining-room table, each with a cup of coffee.

"Well?" he said when he entered.

"The wedding is next month," she said.

"As soon as the holidays are over and the ski crowd goes home," Ty added, "and we can take off on a honeymoon."

Chapter Fourteen

Carly straightened the sweaters and jewelry spilling artfully out of the chest of drawers. The ski resort had been totally full and busy as a beehive during the Christmas holidays. This one tiny shop had done as much business during the same time period as all three of her Chicago ones had done. It had been a good move.

Glancing at the ornamental clocks on one wall, she was glad to see the minute hand inching toward the hour. It was almost ten.

She'd extended the store hours for the brisk holiday business, but she was tired and ready to go home.

A contented sigh escaped her. Home meant Ty and Jonathan and a cup of hot chocolate while they shared a bedtime story. Home meant mad passion and deep contentment, the feeling of belonging.

What had she ever done to deserve this happiness? Sometimes she was afraid it would be snatched away the way her parents had been. But she wouldn't dwell on that. Life could sometimes hurt, but it could also heal. And now…now she was the luckiest person in the world.

She went to close the gate, but another customer entered the shop before she could. She summoned a courteous smile.

The stranger stopped abruptly when he spotted her standing to the side of the tiny store. He was of average height but with the muscles of someone who worked out in a gym rather than one who did real work like a rancher had to.

She glanced at his face. He was probably good-looking for a city fellow. She smiled at her condescending attitude, recalling that she'd been a city gal not too long ago.

"Carly," he said. He had a pleasant voice,

sort of wistful, a little lost. Once that would have appealed to her—

She blinked in confusion. The man standing before her was no stranger. He was her ex-fiancé.

"My gosh," she said, at a total loss to understand his presence. He was more like an apparition than someone she'd once known and thought she loved.

"I've been trying to find you for months." There was a note of accusation and a smidgen of hurt in his tone.

Ah, she thought, the hurt-but-putting-on-a-brave-face act. She was surprised at her cynicism. Little more than two years ago, she'd been completely taken in by his vulnerable air.

"Why?" Her tone was cool, controlled and not very interested in his answer.

Now it was his turn to blink in surprise. She could almost see the wheels turning in his head as he calculated a new strategy. She wondered why she hadn't seen through him from the first.

But then she'd been blinded by her own loneliness, her own need to belong, to have someone of her very own.

"I...we can't let it go like this. Once we had something...." He shook his head as if in despair. "We let it slip away."

"I can't believe this," she murmured. He was better than the leading man in Isa's new play. "Did you ever think of going into the theater?" she inquired politely. "It pays good if you can make it to the top, I understand." Another idea came to her. "In case you need money to pay your attorney fees."

A flush ran into his face.

"Bingo," she said softly, laughing at how gullible she'd once been. She gazed at him in pity. "Go away," she said quite firmly. She showed him her left hand, where Ty's ring sparkled on her finger. "I'm engaged to the man of my dreams. A real man...one who knows what caring for someone else really means, a man I love with all my heart."

"You're acting on the rebound, darling—"

"Don't call me that. On your lips, it's a travesty." She frowned as the multiple clocks struck ten. She was impatient to get home. "On his, it's an endearment. I doubt if you know the difference," she said with a sharpness that surprised both of them.

The stranger who had once presumed to know her intimately hesitated, then the knowledge that he'd failed, that his little-boy-lost appeal wasn't going to work this time, seeped into his eyes, and with it, a meanness she hadn't been aware of.

"You're a cold bitch anyway," he said.

Once that would have hurt. "No," she corrected gently. "I'm not." In Ty's arms, she knew exactly what kind of woman she was.

She wondered if she'd have to yell for security to get rid of him, but he turned and left without a backward glance, his back stiff as if highly insulted.

Off to find the next sucker, she mused with candid self-honesty. She started for the desk to close out her books for the night. A shadow loomed in the doorway.

"Hello, darling," Ty said. He wore a bemused smile, and she knew he'd heard every word.

She stepped into his arms. "My hero." She was laughing when he kissed her.

Ty pulled at his tie and cleared his throat. He was nervous, more than he'd expected to be. Well, it was a big day.

"You look fine, Dad," Jonathan assured him.

"Right," Shane agreed.

Ty looked at his two best men—his son and his brother—and tried to smile. It was an effort.

From the partially open door, he could see the front of the church. Tina was already seated on the family pew with Ian. Mrs. Perkins was with her.

As soon as the preacher reached the dais, it would be time for him and the best men to take their place. Then Carly would come down the aisle with Brody. Her foster brother was the only kin she had at the wedding, although an aunt and uncle had been invited.

He was suddenly glad that she'd had Brody while she was growing up. Carly was a warm, caring woman. She needed a family to love.

He and Jonathan were about to become that family.

That's what made him nervous. He wasn't sure he deserved her. Hell, he knew he didn't. But he'd try. With every ounce of love in him, he'd try to show her how very much she meant to him.

In his first marriage, he'd been an ignorant boy. As a man, he knew how easily things could go wrong. He wouldn't let those things happen with Carly. A man had to remember to communicate his feelings, to tell his woman how necessary she was to him.

Necessary? Carly had become the very center of his life—his friend, his lover, his wildest, deepest joy. Had he told her all that? He would as soon as they were alone....

"Okay," Shane said.

The three of them left the anteroom and joined the pastor at the front of the church. Ty swallowed hard against the knot that collected in his throat while he surveyed the crowded church.

The bridal music started. Isa came down the aisle. Then everyone stood. And there was Carly, as shimmery and ethereal as an angel in her long white gown.

His chest filled with clamoring emotion, squeezing his heart until it felt ready to burst. There was room for only one thing—his love for this woman.

She smiled when she came near. He saw her eyes, dark and mysterious, promising him irresistible passion when they were alone, and with that promise, another...the gift of her love for as long as they lived.

A sense of rightness settled over him. This time was the charm. This time, he'd made the right choice.

He took her hand and turned to the preacher, wanting the man to hurry. He was eager to make his vows.

Carly lay beside her husband. It was dawn, and she wanted to touch him, but she was hesitant about disturbing his sleep. They had a full day and a long trip ahead of them. Their week in Hawaii was at an end. Today they would go home.

It had been a year since they'd been here on a brief but delicious honeymoon. She was glad they'd gotten to return.

"Go ahead," he murmured. "I'm awake."

She snuggled against him, an arm and a leg curled over his chest and thighs. "I love to touch you."

"I like it, too." He settled an arm around

her and pushed up against the pillows. Together they watched the sun rise.

"I can hardly wait to get home."

"Do you miss the shop?"

She laughed. "Hardly. You kept me too occupied. But I miss Jonathan and the walks along the river or the rides up into the mountains. And Tina and Shane and Ian."

"I think you married me for my family," he complained. "But I suppose that's better than for my money, most of which is tied up in the ranch, the orchards and the canning factory."

"No," she said solemnly. "I love *you.* All the rest is nice, like icing, but you're the real part."

She gazed into his eyes and saw contentment in those summery blue depths. He believed her. He trusted her love.

It was a responsibility, she realized—the love of another person. It couldn't be taken lightly or carelessly. She knew how quickly it could be snatched away.

"Don't," Ty said suddenly. He tilted her chin up and studied her face for a long minute.

"This will last," he promised softly. "This love is forever."

Then he kissed her until her blood stirred sweetly through her body and her heart responded, wild in its joy. It was only later that she remembered her news.

"Speaking of family..." She ran her fingertips lightly over his moist torso.

He caught her hand and kissed it, then held it to his chest. "Yes?"

"Ours is going to be increasing." She waited for his reaction. By mutual agreement, they'd left off birth control six months ago.

He pushed himself to an elbow. "Sure?"

"Well, I haven't been to the doctor, but all the signs are, um, propitious."

He laughed and hugged her close. "Jonathan will drive us crazy picking out names. It took him months to decide on 'Ian,' and that was a cousin. A brother or sister will take some major thought. He told me the other day that helping raise a kid was a big responsibility."

"With you for a father, Jonathan for a big brother and Shane and Tina and Ian for kinfolk, I have no doubt that our child will get the best of raising.''

''No doubts at all?'' Ty traced the curve of her jaw, his manner serious and loving.

Carly gazed into eyes as blue as a summer sky. ''No doubts at all,'' she whispered. ''None.''

*   *   *   *   *

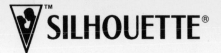

LARGE PRINT TITLES FOR
JULY – DECEMBER 1999

July: A BABY FOR REBECCA — Trisha Alexander
August: MUM FOR HIRE — Victoria Pade
September: LIVE-IN MUM — Laurie Paige
October: THE FATHER NEXT DOOR — Gina Wilkins
November: WAITING FOR NICK — Nora Roberts
December: HOLLY AND MISTLETOE — Susan Mallery

July: EMMETT — Diana Palmer
August: THE TEMPORARY GROOM — Joan Johnston
September: REGAN'S PRIDE — Diana Palmer
October: THE FIVE-MINUTE BRIDE — Leanne Banks
November: THAT BURKE MAN — Diana Palmer
December: RANCHER'S BABY — Anne Marie Winston

Sensation

July: ADDIE AND THE RENEGADE — Dallas Schulze
August: WOMAN WITHOUT A NAME — Emilie Richards
September: PRINCE JOE — Suzanne Brockmann
October: THE LADY IN RED — Linda Turner
November: NIGHTHAWK — Rachel Lee
December: THE BADDEST VIRGIN IN TEXAS — Maggie Shayne